HIT THE DIRT!

"Get back on your horse and ride off this property," the foreman of the Bar D said.

Sam turned and asked Sheriff Cable, "Have I a right to go along with you to search the place?"

Cable was looking past Sam and he said flatly, quickly, "Drop on your belly, Sam!"

Sam didn't hesitate. He fell facedown in Cable's direction. As he hit the dirt and rolled to one side, he heard the flat, close explosion of a rifle. Cable grunted with pain and lurched back in his saddle, his horse dancing to one side.

Sam rolled over on his back, sat up, and saw the smoke rising from the barrel of foreman Shores' rifle. He drew his gun and, without sighting it, fanned the hammer.

Shores' breath escaped him in a savage grunt; he dropped his rifle, his hands went to his belly, and he went down.

Dell books by Luke Short

TROUBLE COUNTRY

LUKE SHORT

A DELL BOOK

Published by
Dell Publishing
a division of
Bantam Doubleday Dell Publishing Group, Inc.
666 Fifth Avenue
New York, New York 10103

ISBN: 0-440-20594-8

Reprinted by arrangement with the author's estate

Printed in the United States of America

Published simultaneously in Canada

November 1990

10 9 8 7 6 5 4 3 2 1

OPM

For Jann Mills

1

Sam Dana reined up his bay on the foothill bench above the Bar D spread that he hadn't seen for more than a year. It could have been the savage, early-afternoon sun battering the old frame house, for in his absence the big old cottonwoods that once shaded it had been cut down. The small fence that surrounded the tiny front yard now guarded a brown, paper-littered weed patch.

Scowling, Sam found the old trail and put his bay down it, still regarding the place. He was a tall man wearing worn range clothes. His lean, flat-cheeked and beard-stubbled face was so weather-browned it made his blue eyes seem almost gray under black tufted eyebrows.

A couple of hundred yards beyond the Big House was the spacious log cabin where his half brother, Walt, five years older than Sam, and his wife, Rita, lived. There were two saddled horses at its small tie rail under a big pine tree and even as he watched he saw two men bolt out the front door and run for the two horses. Even at this distance he could see that neither of them could be Walt. They mounted hurriedly, but instead of heading for the road to Garrison that lay between Walt's and the bunkhouse, they headed for the outlet of the trail he was descending, which ended just short of the horse corral.

The pair of them were waiting on the flats at the end of the trail, both dismounted. One, a squat bulky man of perhaps forty-five, held a carbine cradled in an elbow. The other, taller and younger, looked sullen and tough.

When Sam reined up, facing them, the older man said, "You're lost, stranger. You're on deeded land, so you're trespassing. Go back the way you came."

"Who're you?" Sam asked quietly. "I don't remember you."

"I'm Wiley Shores, and I don't remember you either." He took two steps to his right and studied the brand on Sam's horse, then said, "I don't remember that brand either. So back up the trail you go."

"Is Walt around?" Sam asked.

"Around Garrison somewhere."

Sam inclined his head in the direction of the horse corral. "Duke's in there. Walt always rode him, so he's here. Now, point that rifle toward the ground and stand away."

"Just who do you figure to be, mister?"

"Half owner of the land you're standing on," Sam said. "You're both in my way. Move!"

Sam touched spurs to his horse and the two men parted to let Sam ride between them, headed for the far corrals.

What's wrong here? he wondered. Two new hard-nosed hands who didn't like strangers. In the old days, any visitor was welcome, even if he was only riding the grubline. These two, after he had asserted his half ownership, didn't even greet him or acknowledge they'd heard of him, only let him pass between them.

When he reined in at the corral and secured his bay alongside the other two horses he tramped past the two hands, together now and watching him, and went to the office side door of the Big House, knocked, and stepped inside.

The room, Sam remembered, was a catchall for all the worn-out or unwanted furniture of Bar D. The shabby rolltop desk, the chairs that almost leaked stuffing, and the leather sofa that was boot- and spur-scarred.

The last held the stretched-out form, under a tattered Indian blanket, of Walt Dana, just rousing from sleep. When he sat up, brushing the blanket aside, he recognized Sam, smiled, and heaved his thick bulk erect, saying, "Well, well. The fiddlefoot shows up again."

He was a paunchy bear of a man and, hand held out, he crossed the room and shook hands with Sam.

"Big brother, you're some bigger," Sam said.

Walt ran a meaty hand through thinning sand-colored hair, then slapped his ample belly with the palm of his other hand. "Yeah, that happens to some of us," he said with smug resignation. He moved over to the desk's swivel chair and swung it around to face the easy chair by the door.

Sam sat down in the easy chair, took off his hat, laid it on the floor beside it, and looked carefully at his half brother, not much liking what he saw.

Before he could speak, Walt said, "You're a little late for Mom and Dad's funeral, Sam. I know you couldn't have made it, but you never even answered my letter."

"I never got it. Where'd you send it?"

"San Dimas, Mexico."

Sam sighed, *"New* Mexico, Walt, not Mexico."

"Then how'd you know about the accident?"

"I was out on a prospect. Went into town for supplies. Ran into a man I knew and he told me he read about the train wreck and saw the deathlist in the papers." He paused. "You must have gone through her letters. Enough to know where I was."

"She burned your letters. Remember, she was your mother, not mine. Pa had a poor notion of what you were doin' except prospectin'."

"How's Rita?"

"She's livin' in town. The trees around the house caught a blight and we had to cut 'em down. With no shade the house got hotter than the hinges of hell and she couldn't take it any longer."

Sam only nodded, then asked, "Who's new on the crew? I sure never saw the two that stopped me before."

"The whole crew is new to you. I reckon the old bunch didn't hanker workin' for a younger man. When Pa was killed they quit."

Everything Walt had said so far held a certain reasonableness, but Sam was determined to persist. He said then, "I saw those two that stopped me come out of your place. How come?"

"When we moved in here I told the boys to use it. There's only six of them, countin' the cook. It's closer to me and the barn and corrals. I eat with them, so I see it's taken care of."

Sam picked up his hat and rose. "Well, the place looks like hell, Walt. From the bench trail I saw you had down wire in the horse pasture. I know you've got a new crew, but nobody's riding line. I know these last months have been hard. I know—"

Walt cut in sharply, "You don't know! While you been out lookin' for the Lost Dutchman with your minin'-school brains, I've been runnin' Bar D; *your* half and mine."

"I'm grateful, Walt."

Walt heaved his big body out of his chair and glowered at Sam. "Grateful! You're so damn grateful you'll pull stakes in a few days and be gone for another year or two! I run the spread, boss the crew, and then split with you all the profits I make! It's not good enough, Sam." He moved closer now and his anger was plain on his broad, flushed face. "Since you won't work here and don't give a damn about the place, will you sell your half interest to me? That's as fair as I can put it!"

Sam thought a moment, then said, "I may want to come back here someday, Walt."

"Not with me here you won't. Either you sell out to me, or I sell out to you!"

"What's the whole outfit worth?" Sam asked quietly.

"Ask Wilford at the bank. He's got all the figures and papers."

"I'll do that. I have to go in this afternoon to look up some maps for a couple of days. I'll see him."

"You're welcome to put up right here. We've got room and half the house is yours."

"I reckon not," Sam said. "Town'll save me time."

2

Outside, Sam moved over to his bay, alone now at the corral. Looking over at Walt's house, he saw that the two horses he had tied his next to were now tied under the big pine in front of Walt's house.

Picking up the road to Garrison, he reviewed his welcome "home." To begin with, the spread wasn't being worked, it was being guarded. Why? From any strange rider like himself, obviously. And he couldn't blame Walt for resenting the fact that, as half owner, he ran Bar D but had to split all profits with the absentee owner of the other half. His ultimatum to sell him his half or buy Walt's half made a kind of sense too. But Walt was lazy and incompetent, even as a young man, sure to fail at anything he tried.

There *was* something wrong here, and he had to find out exactly what.

Garrison, so named because it had once been a temporary tent-town army post, was now the county seat of Campbell County. From its wide main street, flanked with false-front frame-and-brick buildings, Sam could see the towering Bradbury Mountains to the west, which he had been traveling through the past three days.

He passed the brick courthouse at the edge of town, joined the busy Saturday mid-afternoon wagon traffic, passed the two-story Garrison House, and put in at the feed stable a block beyond. There he left his bay, and took his blanket roll and left it at the hotel, where he signed for a room. Afoot on the boardwalk, he headed upstreet, turned into a sidestreet, then angled across it and headed for a one-story frame building.

It had a window on either side of a half-glassed door whose upper half bore, in discreet white lettering, the legend CYRUS F. ALLEN, and below this, ATTORNEY AT LAW.

Sam opened the door into the familiar waiting room, saw that the office door in the rear wall was open.

He called, "I can lick any judge in that office!"

There was a pause and then a shout of laughter came from the office. "You always could, you damned bully!"

They met in the middle of the waiting room to shake hands; tall, lean Sam and short, pear-shaped, and bespectacled Cy, whose thinning curly hair was the color of peach fuzz.

"Get my letter of congratulations?" Sam asked.

"I did. And thank you. Before I could answer it the train wreck happened. I'm truly miserably sorry about that, Sam. They were my friends. It was a hell of a way for them to die." He gestured with his head. "Let's go back in my office before someone comes in." After waving Sam into the spacious office whose walls were lined with book-laden shelves, he closed the door and gestured to the leather-covered easy chair facing one side of the desk. Sam took off his hat and seated himself; Cy slid into his own chair behind the flat-topped, paper-littered desk.

"I lost your letter. I tried to get your address from Walt so I could answer it, but he didn't know it—or claimed he didn't." He leaned back in his chair. "Now catch me up on you."

"Well, I finally struck it, Cy. You'll never guess what."

"Gold? Silver? Or both?"

"Coal. What looks like a mountain of it." He went on to tell of his prospect, the last drifting, and finally his approach to Rocky Mountain Central Railroad. They sent in crews to verify what he'd claimed and found it better than anyone expected. Sam refused to sell and settled for an enormous finder's fee and lease with tonnage royalties. He refused a good job offer; he was not hankering for a desk job. The railroad had already started a spur line to the field.

When he finished Cy said, laughing with pleasure, "I knew something like this would happen. You're too damn stubborn for it not to."

"You're the only one I've told, Cy. The word'll get out, but let someone else tell you. Can you be a county judge and still be my case field lawyer?"

"There's nothing against it and I accept with pleasure."

Sam reached out and they shook hands on it. Then Sam said, "That's only part of why I was anxious to see you. The other is, what's happened to Walt and Bar D?"

"If you hadn't brought that up, I intended to," Cy said grimly. "Why do you ask?"

Sam described his homecoming, starting with his being stopped by the hardcases of the new crew and ending with Walt's ultimatum: " 'Sell out to me or buy me out.' What's happened?"

Cy didn't even take time to reflect. "To begin with, the old crew didn't quit, they were fired by Walt. He brought in the roughs. The first ones he brought in got into so much trouble they couldn't buy a drink in any saloon except Albies', the worst."

"But why the rough crew on our place? Who were we fighting?"

"Nobody. Everybody was fighting you because you were stealing their beef, driving them over the mountains and selling to a crooked Indian agent with a forged bill of sale."

"What about the sheriff?"

"Hell, your dad got him elected. Cable isn't going after Walt. He has a debt to pay off to the Danas. Mind you, this is saloon and cardtable talk. I know nothing first-hand, but I think the talk is true."

Sam was silent for a few moments, pondering this. He said at last, "Cy, I'm not going to hang around here trying to reform Walt. It's too late."

"If you do stay you'll be dead in a couple of months," Cy said quietly.

"You mean Walt would kill me? No."

"He wouldn't have to. You two would quarrel and Walt would badmouth you to the crew. They'd get the drift and set up a bushwhack. Both Danas have a bad name now. The shooting would be blamed on the men Walt's stolen cows from. Since you're half owner of Bar D, you presumably knew what was going on and approved. That'll be the story, but you'll be dead."

Again Sam reflected, not liking the obvious which he had not put into words: "So I sell out to Walt and drift."

"You said you don't want to stay. So sell your half to Walt, but not for what it's worth. Say for half its appraised value. I'll find out what that is at the bank."

Sam scowled. "Why?"

"Same reason. You won't be killed if the price is cheap and you clear out so you're not in Walt's way."

"I've never run from anything," Sam said gruffly, then added, "especially from that slob."

Cy frowned and clasped his pudgy white hands on the desk top. "With this coal find as you described it, you won't be short for money up to the day you die. Then why not duck out at a sacrifice you can afford?"

"It's the principle of the thing," Sam growled.

"Principles can get you killed sometimes, and this is one of those times." Cy grinned, then, "What I'm saying is, I want you to come to my funeral, but I don't want to go to yours this soon."

As Sam walked the couple of blocks to the courthouse, he turned over in his mind the advice Cy Allen had given him. While it made Cy's kind of sense, it somehow angered him and gave him a vague feeling of shame even thinking about it. The image of a scared dog, running away with his tail between his legs, came to his mind as he climbed the courthouse steps and went inside.

There was an office on each side of the short corridor that emerged on a long cross-corridor which ran the length of the building. Sam turned left and then headed for the corner room on his right, which he remembered was the office of the county treasurer, so marked by a sign, gilt letters on black background, that thrust at a right angle into the corridor over an open doorway.

It was a small room with a high counter on the right; from the counter rose a ceiling-high, chastely ornate metal grille anchored to the ceiling. It had two customer openings in it and Sam thought *Protect the money, like any bank,* and walked to the nearest window.

Through the grille he saw a young woman rise from behind a paper-strewn, flat-top desk by the open vault door and approach his window. She halted and Sam regarded her swiftly. She could have been in her middle twenties; her hair was ash-blond, her eyes so dark a brown they seemed black. Her wide mouth had a faint lift at the corners, a beginning smile of polite welcome.

"My name's Sam Dana," Sam began. "I'm half owner of—"

"The Bar D," the young woman said. "I trailed you a few grades in school. My name is Sistie Cable."

"Sheriff Morton Cable's girl. I remember you. A long-legged girl with blond pigtails." He looked at her carefully now and saw a full-bodied young woman wearing a white shirtwaist and black full skirt. Her pleasant, wide-mouthed face was faintly freckled and her dark brown eyes under piled-up tawny hair regarded him with a curiosity equal to his own.

Sam grinned and said, "There've been some changes made."

She flushed slightly, gave a low laugh, and said, "Well, girls do grow up, just like boys."

Sam smiled. "How's your dad? I'm going to stop by and see him when I get through here."

"He'll be out of town for a couple of days. Some sort of trouble over in Pleasant Valley. What was it you wanted, Sam?"

"A look at your tax records to see what Bar D is appraised at."

"That's odd. Your brother with two of his men was in about fifteen minutes ago asking for a look at the same thing."

"Not so odd. One of us is going to sell out to the other; likely, me."

"Who is your lawyer? Cy Allen, Howard Olsen, or Peter O'Hara?"

"Cy Allen, of course."

Sistie shrugged. "Why not sell? You're hardly ever here."

She turned, went over to her desk, picked up a heavy record book, and brought it back to the counter window. She pointed to the back of the room on Sam's side. "There's a table and chair back there in case you hadn't noticed."

Sam nodded and reached for the record book when Sistie put a restraining hand on the big volume. "Ever looked at one of these, Sam?" When he shook his head in negation, she said, "Don't believe what you read about property evaluations. They're way, way too low. That's because two of the three commissioners are ranchers. They don't believe in high taxes, so they order the land appraised at about a quarter of what it's worth, or even less. It doesn't even approximate the true market value, so don't be guided by it."

"That's good to know. And thank you." Then he asked with open curiosity, "How did a woman get elected treasurer?"

"Heavens, I'm not the treasurer! I'm a hired deputy. Mr. Balcomb is the elected treasurer. He's old and mostly sick and out of the office. I'm just a hired hand."

"But you do the work," Sam said.

"The work he taught me how to do."

"Good girl." Sam picked up the record book and took it over to the table under the window, pulled out the chair and sat down.

He had no trouble finding the pages listing *Bar D, Charles P. Dana, owner,* because Sistie had marked the page with a folded piece of paper, undoubtedly for Walt earlier.

Sam learned that two sections of grazing land and two residences with auxiliary buildings had an appraised value of three thousand dollars. Sam smiled at this absurdity, but he realized that it worked in his favor in dealing with Walt.

He rose, closed the file book, and headed for the counter window just as a man left it whom he hadn't even heard enter. Sistie saw him and came up to the window as he moved the volume toward her.

"Ridiculous, isn't it?" she said.

"Well, if Bar D is an example, it's a book of fairy tales."

Sistie laughed softly. "And, like fairy tales, nobody believes them." Then a certain soberness came to her face. "The bank has loaned money to your father. I've heard

Pa say so. You'd get a fair, quick appraisal from Mr. Wilford, wouldn't you?"

"That's where I'm headed. Thanks for the help, Sistie, and I'll be seeing you."

Out in the hall, Sam saw that while it was near closing time, all the offices were open and the county clerk's office was crowded. He remembered then that these same commissioners who had ordered low property-tax appraisals had also ordered a working Saturday for county employees in order to accommodate the one-day-in-town-a-week ranch people.

On the boardwalk outside, Sam saw the buckboards and wagons heading out of town, trying to make it home to supper before dark. At Garrison House he took his blanket roll to his front ground-floor room. The noise from the bar at the far end of the corridor reached as far as his room.

As he stripped off his shirt and washed his upper body he reflected on what a strange day this had been. Except for Sistie Cable, it was like coming from sunlight into semidarkness; caution said *Watch your step. It's not like it used to be.*

Clean shirt on, he strapped on his gunbelt, put on his stetson, then headed down the corridor for the noisy barroom. Halting just inside the crowded room, he saw that the long bar on his left was jammed two-deep and all the chairs of the gambling tables, except for a lone poker game, were occupied by drinking men.

Seeing a man at the bar put down his glass and turn to leave, Sam moved into the slot he vacated. One of the eight bartenders, alert to the empty glass before Sam, moved over and said, "What was it, friend?"

"Not mine," Sam said. "I want a labeled whiskey and water."

He got his drink, tasted it, nodded to the bartender,

and paid. Afterward, he picked up his drink and, turning to face the room, put his elbows on the bar and observed the crowd. He was aware now of a man standing at a table where others were seated. He waved and gestured with a "come over" sign and Sam suddenly realized that it was Walt signaling to him.

Taking his drink with him, he moved past the tables and he saw Walt speak to the seated punchers at his table; they rose and were leaving as Sam reached the table.

"Brought your own," Walt observed. "Siddown. We got a lot to chew over in private." His heavy face was flushed and Sam guessed he had come straight here from the courthouse. Walt poured himself a drink from the bottle in front of him and sampled it.

Sam said dryly, "In private, like here."

"There's nothin' more private than a crowd. That's what the pickpockets say."

Sam smiled wryly. "All right. Let's talk private. About what?"

"You selling me your half of Bar D." Sam only nodded, and Walt went on, "I got the county's appraisal of Bar D this afternoon. Know what it is?"

There came an added racket in the room as several men at the biggest card table slid their chairs back and rose and scattered.

When the din diminished Sam said, "Yes, I know what it is. Three thousand dollars."

Walt nodded. "Half of that is fifteen hundred. That's what I'll pay for your half of Bar D."

"You said to me 'buy or sell,' " Sam said slowly. "What if I decide to buy? Still fifteen hundred for your half?"

"Times twenty," Walt said flatly. "The place is worth sixty thousand. If you can dig up thirty thousand cash, it's yours."

"Why the difference when you sell?"

"Because I damned well earned the difference!" Walt said angrily. "I told you. While you were batting around with a prospector's pick, I worked the place, and damned hard! There should be a difference."

"You're right," Sam said, nodding. "Pay me fifteen hundred and I'll sign over my half to you."

The flush of anger in Walt's face gave way to a look of incredulity. "I don't believe you."

"I'll have Cy draw up the papers."

Walt smiled and said, "At last you're lookin' at my side of it."

A man approached their table and halted; Sam recognized him only after Walt said, "Hi, Les. How you been?"

Uninvited, Les Beecham pulled out a chair and sat down. He was Sam's age and height, leaned to a tough gauntness. A full, fawn-colored mustache drooped at the corners of his wide mouth, and green eyes above a thin, high-bridged nose were cold, without friendliness. He thumbed his hat back on his forehead, then folded his hands on the table, looking from Walt to Sam, then back to Walt.

Beecham said then in a neutral tone of voice, "Been waitin' to catch you two together because you're the Bar D owners."

"*Were* the owners," Sam said, and nodded to Walt. "There's the sole owner."

"How long since?" Beecham demanded.

"Five minutes ago, or until you butted in," Walt said.

"All right, Walt. I'll give it to you with the bark on. Before I do, I'll tell you I'm not packin' a gun. Five of my friends are. Two of them are watchin' your men. Three of them are watchin' you. Don't make a quick move."

"Why should I?" Walt asked.

"Because I'm namin' you and your crew a bunch of cattle rustlers."

Walt straightened up, kept his hands on the table, and looked at Sam, who was observing him with interest. Walt's attention returned to Beecham.

"That's a damned lie! If it's true, prove it!"

"I already have," Beecham said. "A couple of us you've been raidin' went over to the reservation on beef-issue days. The issue corral had some of our stuff in it. We checked with the agent and looked at the bills of sale. Our names were right, but the signatures were forged."

"Hell, any cow thief with a band book could do that," Walt said scornfully.

"But the writin' on all the bills of sale was the same—one man. You."

"How do you know my writin'?"

"You buy from a half a dozen stores in town and sign for it. I checked your signatures. Your capital *D* in *Dana* isn't connected with the *A* that follows it. Right?"

"Is there any law against that?"

"You stole some of Don Danfelser's cows. On the bills of sale supposedly signed by Don, your *D*'s are not connected with the next letter. Don signs his name with the *D* connected." Beecham stood up. "Let's go out in the street. We're gonna need room." He looked at Sam then. "Not your fight, Sam, so don't get yourself hurt. You were away when all of this happened."

Walt gave Sam a baleful glance as if he knew what was coming, unstrapped his gunbelt and laid it on the table, then rose and fell in behind Beecham, who was heading for the street door. Sam took off his gunbelt too, then took both gunbelts to a vigilant houseman at the head of the bar, asking, "Could you watch these for a while?"

The houseman nodded, took the belts, and hung them on coathooks on the sidewall. As Sam headed for the street door he thought about what Beecham had just said to Walt. Rita had caught on to Walt's rustling; wanted no part of it and had left him.

Out on the boardwalk, he saw immediately that several punchers had ducked under the horse-lined tie rails and were heading for the middle of the street. Sam found a break in the tie rail and saw Walt and Les Beecham, their hats discarded now, fists up and facing each other, making a slow circle in the middle of the dusty street.

Sam judged that Walt outweighed Les by a good fifty pounds and was taller. It didn't seem an even match, but Beecham had asked for the fight.

Now Beecham stopped his circling and moved in. Before Walt could raise his heavy arms, Les gave him an open-handed belt across the mouth and a raking, fisted back-hand across the nose before he back-pedaled away from Walt's certain charge. When it came with a shout of anger, Les sidestepped and tripped him purposely. Walt crashed into the dust, facedown; almost at the instant he hit, before he could react, Les was astride him, pinning him and scooping dust into his face for seconds. Then he rolled away and came to his feet.

With a roar of curses Walt lurched to his feet, trying to rub the dust out of his eyes and succeeding only in rubbing it in.

Les didn't hesitate to take advantage. Walt's hands were busy, with his arms momentarily useless, and Beecham moved into him, driving a fist into the blubbery bulge of his belly. Walt's exploding breath was a near shout and the circle of watchers yelled derisively. Walt swung a wild, backhanded, clubbing blow that caught Beecham on the cheek and sent him sprawling in the dust on his back. Then Walt bent over, arms wrapped around his middle, gagging for breath.

Beecham scrambled to his feet and charged, then drove

blow after blow into Walt's unprotected and contorted face. A roundhouse swing caught Walt's shelving jaw; he toppled over on his side and then rolled on his back, and was still.

The crowd cheered as Beecham, steady on his feet, began to beat the dust from his pants. The two Bar D hands came over to Walt, followed by their watchers.

Beecham looked at the crowd, then said, "If Cable won't arrest a cow thief, then maybe this is just as good."

Sam left the group of witnesses to Walt's beating, picked up his gun from the houseman, and walked through the almost empty saloon to his room.

He tossed the gunbelt on the bed in a gesture of disgust, rammed his hands in his hip pockets, and began to pace the length of the room. Walt had not only been named a rustler and taken a deserved beating, but he had dragged the good name of Dana into his muck.

Then Sam halted abruptly. *If I go through with this deal with Walt, I'm running,* he thought sourly. Running where? Out of here and on another mine prospect, when he already had a strike that would support him the rest of his life?

Right here and now was the problem to face. Bar D had been his life for most of his life. Was he going to turn his back on it, leaving it in the hands of a crook who before he wound up dead or in jail would have lost Bar D?

No. In spite of Cy's warning to sell cheap and get out of here, if he wanted to live, he was not going to do it. Cy's advice made a kind of sense, but not his own kind of sense.

He was staying.

3

As he rode closer to the Diamond B, Sam began to remember the Beecham place. A big log house under giant cottonwoods, parents long gone, three brothers, Buff and Pete both much older than Les, who was just over thirty.

Sam headed for one of the cottonwoods on the mountain side of the house, which was studded with tie rings. Dismounted, Sam headed for the front porch and saw Buff, the graying, heavyset, oldest son, rise out of a deep porch chair and stand at the head of the two porch steps.

As Sam approached, Buff grinned. "Sam Dana, ain't it? You sure ain't cricket-size anymore."

Sam laughed, came up the two steps, and they shook hands.

"Lookin' for Les, ain't you? Trouble?"

"If he's around, Buff. No trouble at all. Just talk."

Buff stroked his beard-stubbled square chin reflectively. "Well, I don't know how he got home last night. The whole damn town must have bought him drinks."

"They should have. It was something to see. I've wanted to do that for a long time."

Buff nodded. "Me too. Sit down, Sam. I'll see if he's alive."

A couple of minutes later Les walked out onto the porch with a drink of whiskey in each hand. Sam came out of his chair; they looked at each other and Sam laughed. Les grinned wryly and extended a glass.

"I don't often drink alone, Sam, but last night I wish I had."

"A public celebration, Les. Overdue."

"You're not mad, then?"

"A little, but only because I didn't do it."

They both sat down in hide easy chairs and, facing each other, lifted their glasses in silent toast and drank. Les said then, "Where have I tasted this stuff before?" Then he added, "If you ain't mad, Sam, then why this welcome Sunday visit? Forget to tell me somethin' yesterday?"

Sam shook his head. "No. To correct something I did tell you." He paused to isolate what was coming next. "I'm not selling out to Walt. I'm going to try and buy him out of Bar D. Try, hell, I'm *going* to. What's it worth, Les?"

Les frowned in thought then and was silent, thinking. Then he said, "If I had thirty thousand I'd offer it. But you already own half of it, so cut that figure in two. You got fifteen thousand, or can you get it?"

"I've got it," Sam said, and he told Les about discovering the coal field up north and leasing it to the railroad on a tonnage royalty and a finder's fee. Les could not disguise his pleasure and surprise at Sam's news.

"If you've got the money, buy him out," Les said.

"But his price for Bar D isn't yours, Les, it's double."

Les put his glass on the porch floor beside him and said slowly, "To buy his half it costs you thirty thousand." He shook his head. "Not worth it, Sam."

"I'm on my way to tell him so."

"Yesterday you said you'd sold your half. Now you want to buy his half. What happened?"

"You," Sam answered. "When I told you in the barroom I'd sold out to Walt, it was true. I intended to. After you named him, chapter and verse, then beat hell out of him before half the town, I changed my mind. Dana has always been a good name here. I want it to be again. That's why I want Bar D, all of it."

"Sounds like you. How can I help?"

"You mean that? Because if you do, you can help one hell of a lot," Sam said. When Les nodded, Sam went on, "Come with me to see Walt."

"Now?" At Sam's nod, Les grinned. "You tryin' to get me blown out of my saddle?"

"Then bring along Buff and Pete. Walt's rustling hurt them as much as it did you."

"Too right," Les said. He rose and headed back into the house.

Ten minutes later the four of them set out for Bar D. All had rifles in their saddle scabbards except for Sam. There wasn't much talk on the way but Sam had the feeling that the two older Beechams were looking forward to a sort of showdown.

Sam knew that Cy Allen would wildly disagree with what he was about to do and say but he had settled that with himself last night. This was the time to tackle Walt, when he was beat up and mad and wondering what was going to happen next.

At Bar D, Sam put his horse straight for the corner office; he rode ahead, hoping that one of the riffraff crew would identify him before warning them off. Two men emerged from Walt's house, but only stood by the door, rifles in hand, watching.

As he approached the office Wiley Shores stepped out, pretended he had just seen them, and halted, his hands dropping to his belt, close to his gun.

Sam reined in and Shores asked in a surly voice, "What do *you* want?"

Sam swung out of the saddle and faced him. "I want

you out of the way or I'll walk over you. Now get back to your kennel."

"Walt's hurtin'. He can't see no one."

"One man's opinion. Get out of my way!"

Shores looked past him and Sam heard footsteps behind him. That would be Les, Sam guessed, and he was sure of it when Shores stepped aside, shrugged, turned, and headed for Walt's small house. Les stopped beside Sam, rifle dangling from his fist. Sam said, "Better let me go in alone, Les. I'll call you. Get a horse between you and him. I don't know how crazy he is. He might shoot through a window."

"I come in without a gun, you said."

"I'll keep mine." Sam turned, moved to the office door, knocked, and shoved the door open. Walt was in front of the desk, gun leveled.

"Why'd you bring him?" Walt growled. "I'll kill him!"

Sam only shook his head. "You're in enough trouble without that. Put it away."

Walt's shirt held the stains of dried blood. His heavy face was bruised and swollen, one eye almost closed, a healing gash on his left jaw. Sam guessed that, arriving here after the fight, he had been led to bed and had slept through until noon.

Walt suddenly put down his gun on the desk and asked, "Just why in hell did you bring him here? So he could crow?"

"No. He'll be a witness to what we said yesterday and will say today. The only witness."

When Walt only grunted, Sam turned, opened the door, and beckoned to Les, who left his brothers, tramped over, and entered the office.

Neither he nor Walt spoke, nor did they even acknowledge each other's presence. Sam closed the door, waved Les to the chair beside it, then crossed over to the easy chair on the other side of the window. Walt sat down in the swivel chair, turned it to face Sam, and sullenly waited for Sam to speak.

Sam said, "Les, when you came over to our table yesterday, you said you were glad the owners of the Bar D were there together, so you could talk to us both." At Les's nod, Sam asked, "What did I say?"

"You said Walt was sole owner. You'd sold out your half to him five minutes ago."

Sam looked at Walt. "I've changed my mind. I'm not selling to you. You said, 'Sell to me or buy me out.' I'm buying you out."

Walt's face was a study of baffled rage. "What changed your mind?"

Sam leaned forward, elbows on knees. "You did, after Les beat you up and named you a rustler to the crowd."

"What if I won't sell? You changed your mind. Why can't I?"

"You'll sell." Sam's tone of voice was cold. "You're through here, Walt. Once a Cattlemen's Association detective hits the reservation and looks at the bills of sale, you'll be arrested. Also it'll be open season on you for all the owners you've stolen from. If you had any sense you'd be on your way now."

Walt regarded him with purest hatred. "You like this, don't you?"

"No. I just like the good name of Dana. You don't."

Walt hauled himself to his feet, fury in his flushed face. He took two steps toward the battered couch, almost fell, then stumbled back and sagged into the swivel chair again.

"All right. Come up with the figure I named yesterday —thirty thousand cash—and I'll sign."

"Half that, a fair price. And don't talk about the work

you've done outside of forging bills of sale. It doesn't show."

"You haven't got fifteen thousand in cash," Walt said roughly. "Where's it at?"

"In the Bank of Garrison." Sam stood up. "I'll give you tomorrow morning to hunt up a lawyer to draw up the deed. Bring it to me at the hotel. That'll include all cattle and horses branded Bar D. You can keep two horses of your choice and personal possessions. I'll want you and your riffraff off Bar D by sundown Tuesday. If you're not, I'll move you."

Walt sneered, "One-man army."

Les spoke up now after a long but alert silence, "Let's make that a twenty-man *posse,* not a one-man army, Sam."

Walt looked from Les to Sam, then heaved himself to his feet. He said then in mock terror, "Gee. I better pack up." He limped to the door beside the desk that opened into the rest of the house, opened it, went through the doorway, and slammed the door shut with a thundering crash.

The two men grinned at each other. Les said, "Sit down, Sam. Let's chew this over." When Sam seated himself Les asked, "Reckon he's listenin'?"

"What if he is?"

"All right. What about a crew?"

"I hadn't thought of it, Les. I'll look around."

"You been gone too long. Let me look. Thought about a foreman?"

"I've got one in mind, but I don't think he'd leave where he is."

"Who?"

"You," Sam said.

Les's jaw dropped and then his tawny mustache lifted

at the corners in a smile. "I wasn't fishin' for that, Sam. I was tryin' to look ahead some."

"Sound good?" At Les's affirmative nod Sam asked, "Is that going to leave you Beechams shorthanded?"

"Every time I'm in town somebody hits me for work. No."

Sam stood up, and now Les did too. "You're the ramrod. Like you said, I've been away from this too long. You set the crew's wages and your own salary. Make it a good one, because you'll be earning every damned penny of it."

Now Sam crossed over to Walt's desk, pulled open the lower drawer, and lifted out an unopened bottle of whiskey and put it on the desk. "Whistle Buff and Pete in here, Les. We're goin' to drink to this even if we drink out of the bottle."

4

It was just after eleven o'clock Monday morning when Walt, followed by his crew of five, moved into the Garrison House bar. Save for Sam, who was nursing a beer on a barstool at the bar, the two bartenders and the houseman were the only occupants of the room. Walt's crew, headed by Shores, stopped at the nearest barstools, a seedy-looking lot of nameless, unshaven, womanless men.

Walt's bruised face looked a little less swollen than it had yesterday, but the bruises had darkened; he had changed to an equally dirty shirt as he had worn yesterday, but this one was not bloodstained.

He took a stool beside Sam and without a word of greeting he said, "I got to thinkin'. Is the bank going to have fifteen thousand cash on hand?"

"They have. I asked Jess Wilford if he could come up with it by noon. He said yes."

"He better or I'll tear up the deed I got in my pocket."

"Who did it?"

"Fellow name of Olsen. You don't know him."

Sam finished his beer and stood up. "Let's go show it to Cy."

"Let's let the boys finish their beer."

Sam sat down again, saying, "Scared without your bodyguards?"

"You said I oughta be," Walt growled.

"So I did. So you should be." Sam was tempted to ask what Walt's plans were, but he really didn't care. Besides, if he was asked about his plans he would lie, Sam was sure.

Presently Walt stood up and headed for the street, Sam trailing. Walt's crew followed them out. Once on the boardwalk, two of the crew got in front of them and the other three fell in behind them. On the way to the corner, every man they passed got a careful scrutiny from six pairs of eyes.

This strange-appearing group had barely hauled up before Cy's door when it opened and Cy escorted an elderly woman onto the boardwalk and bid her goodbye. When Cy spotted Sam he smiled in greeting.

"Anyone else in your office, Cy?" Walt asked.

"I'm alone. Come in."

Walt nodded to Shores and the bodyguards spread out up and down the walk. In the waiting room, Cy shook hands with Sam and ignored Walt.

"What can I do for the Danas? Tell me in my office." He led the way into his office and motioned them to the two easy chairs flanking his desk.

Cy looked from Walt to Sam, his round face reflecting a wary puzzlement. "What's this, Sam?"

"I want you to check a deed, Cy. Show him, Walt."

Walt took off his hat, pulled a folded sheet of paper from its crown, put the paper in front of Cy, then put his hat back on. Immediately Sam took off his hat and put it on the floor beside his chair.

Cy unfolded the deed, read it, gave Sam a despairing glance, then reread it. Finally, he asked of Sam, "Have you read it?" When Sam shook his head, Cy slid the deed over to him. Sam read it, then, like Cy, reread it, and slid it back over to Cy. "That was our agreement. Is it bullet-proof?"

"Yes, Olsen's a good lawyer, and a careful man. If

O'Hara had drawn it up, I'd have asked for a day to sit on it. Have you got the money?"

Sam reached into his shirt pocket, drew out a folded check, and put it beside the deed. Cy looked at it, said, "Cashier's check, same as gold," and shoved the check in front of Walt. "That wraps it up, wouldn't you say?"

Walt picked up the check, examined it, and said, "I'd say so," then put it into his shirt pocket.

Cy said, "If you'll excuse us, Walt, Sam and I have unfinished business to talk over."

Walt rose, said, "So long," and left the room without so much as a look at Sam, closing the door behind him.

Cy leaned back in his chair and regarded Sam with growing disapproval. He said then, "You don't need a lawyer, Sam, you need a keeper."

"It's possible," Sam conceded.

"Possible, hell! You've proven it. Why pay me for advice when all you do is go against it? You could be out of this mess with a financial sacrifice. Instead of that, you just bought the whole damned mess."

"You hear about Les Beecham beating Walt Saturday, naming him a rustler?"

"I heard about it from a dozen people. You could have been out of town and away from it before it ever happened."

"No," Sam said. He told of Beecham's talk with Walt in the saloon. Les had proof of Walt's rustling, named the proof, picked the fight, and beat up Walt, afterward naming him to the crowd. He finished by saying, "I'm proud of the name Dana. Damned if I'll slink off and leave it lying here in manure. I want to make it what it was. So would you, Cy."

Cy nodded slowly, then sighed. "I guess I would. Where's Walt going?"

"Don't know and I don't care." Then he told of hiring

Les Beecham as foreman, who would round up a crew. Walt had until sundown tomorrow to get off Bar D with his outlaw crew.

"Better and better," Cy said, "but don't start thinking you're shut of him."

"How so?"

"You cut his asking price in half and you've hired a foreman that licked him. Just watch it, Sam."

From across Main Street, Les Beecham watched Walt Dana leave Cy Allen's office and pick up his bodyguards. They walked as far as the corner, turned left, and went into the brick corner building which housed the Bank of Garrison. That meant, Les knew, that the check for Bar D had been delivered and was about to be cashed.

Les went back to his horse, mounted, and headed up the street for the courthouse. He wondered idly what Walt was going to do with Sam's money. There was enough of it to buy a small spread if he wanted one; but did he? Les wondered.

He tied his horse along some others at the courthouse tie rail, went inside, and turned right down the long corridor, passed the commissioner's empty room, and walked through the open doorway of Sheriff Cable's office.

There were two desks in the big corner room, and the sheriff was seated at the bigger one by a west window. At the sound of footsteps in the room, Sheriff Cable swiveled his chair and rose out of it. He was a tall man with thick, iron-gray hair and mustache. Behind steel-rimmed glasses his brown eyes held a friendly wariness as becomes a man who is uncertain of what is coming next.

They shook hands and Les asked, "Have a good trip, Sheriff?"

Sheriff Cable waved him to the chair beside his and Les sat down, thumbing back his hat.

"Hell, no sheriff has good trips, except getting home." He regarded Les now with a veiled amusement. "Perry tells me you got some exercise out front of the hotel Saturday."

"Not much, but that's partly why I'm here. I got fed up with our beef being sold to the Indian agent but not gettin' paid for it."

"It's not in my county, Les."

"But the beef is from your county. I can prove it." He told then of the forged bills of sale that Walt or one of his crew presented to the agent and collected on. He told of verifying Walt's handwriting on the bills from his accounts in town.

"Go to the Cattlemen's Association if you have proof," the sheriff said. "Let them file charges."

"Why haven't you gone to them?" Les countered.

"Because I don't have proof, like you say you do. You say that's only partly why you're here. What else?"

"You'll hear it damn quick. Sam Dana bought out Walt's share of Bar D this morning. I'm Sam's foreman now. I'm hirin' a new crew, and we take over tomorrow at sundown."

Cable smiled. "I'm glad to hear that. Sam was always my favorite Dana boy, even if he was a fiddlefoot. I thought Walt was aimin' to buy Sam's half."

"It didn't work out that way," Les said. And then he asked abruptly, "Any chance of you deputizin' me, Mort?"

The sheriff's eyes widened in astonishment. "On what grounds?"

"I want to be able to arrest a man, since you won't do it."

"You're talkin' about Walt, aren't you?"

"Walt or any of his crew."

"They have to be caught in the act, with the evidence. Are you talking about Diamond B cattle?"

"I'm talkin' about Bar D beef," Les said flatly.

"Steal his own cattle? Make sense, man."

"They're not his beef anymore. They're Sam's. And hell yes, he'd steal from his brother—or me or you, if you had any cattle. You've guaranteed he can get away with it."

Cable flushed at this series of open accusations. Now he rose and made a slow circle of the big room. Les watched him until he came to a halt before him.

"Where's Walt headed for?"

"He hasn't said."

"He could be leavin' the county. If I deputized you, which I won't, your power of arrest would be confined to Campbell County only. I can't do it, Les."

Now Les came to his feet. "I've paid an Indian stable hand to watch the beef issue on the reservation. If any Bar D stuff shows up there, I'll head for Walt."

"Anybody can forge a signature on a bill of sale."

"Nobody has on Bar D stuff. So, I'm tellin' you."

Without another word Les walked out.

5

When the Bar D crew reached the spread, Walt said to Shores, "Come over to the office with me, Wiley. We got medicine to make."

They separated from the crew and headed for the office, dismounted, and went inside. Walt threw his hat on the desk and took his swivel chair. Shores sat in the chair by the door, hat on.

"Got to talkin' with Wilford at the bank," Walt said. "You saw me. Asked him if he knew of a small place I could get cheap. He's holdin' paper on old Pemberton's place and is about to foreclose. Know it?"

"Circle P. I know it. Rundown and damn little graze, all of it poor," Shores said.

"Well, the house will keep us out of the weather. Ride over and ask him what he'll take for it. Don't say I sent you. Tell him you want to set up for yourself."

"Soon's I eat, I'm on my way. That all?"

"No. Tell the boys to pack their gear this afternoon and head for the Brush Creek line camp. After you see Pemberton, you go there too. I'll be there after dark."

Mild surprise showed on Shores' face. "You said we got until sundown tomorrow to move."

"Why stay another day? Hell, I'm paid. Soon's I go through some papers, I'm through."

"Want a wagon or a buckboard?"

"It'll all go in a saddlebag," Walt said.

Shores nodded and rose. "Let's go eat."

Shores left and Walt leaned back in his chair, staring out the window at nothing. Patiently he reviewed the events of these last three days in which his fortunes had fallen from an all-time high to a lifetime low. True, he had come out of it with a comfortable stake, but he had taken a humiliating beating, had openly been called a thief, was landless and without property, and was wifeless and childless. Most of this hard luck was thanks to shiftless Sam Dana, brother in name only.

He rose now and opened the door beside the desk, which led to the dining room. It was full of stiff, silly chairs around a big table. Open cupboards against the walls held dishes and glassware. There was nothing here he wanted or could use. Afterward, he moved through the wide arch into the parlor. It was the same story here. There was the same useless furniture he didn't want and had never owned.

He crossed the hall corridor and didn't bother looking in the sewing room. Rita had already cleaned it out. His father's den behind it held a desk and easy chair, both useless, as were the crossed sabers on the wall and crossed Civil War muskets on the other. The locked bookcases held only books of history, which didn't interest him, and Sam's mining textbooks he couldn't understand.

The climb to the second floor stretched every sore muscle Les Beecham had touched. Walt rested halfway up the stairs, then climbed to the second floor, passed the closed doors of two bedrooms, and walked through the doorway of the third room. It held a stench of sweat and unwashed socks that Walt wasn't aware of.

He went over to the clothes-littered, unmade bed and lay down on it. In minutes he was asleep. Nothing he had seen on his tour did he want to keep nor did he value. All of them were mementos of a father who had quietly held him in contempt and a stepmother who had openly disliked him.

He slept for three hours, wakened refreshed, rummaged around his closet, and found several dirty shirts. His blanket roll was in a corner of his closet and he unrolled it and wrapped the shirts in it. Afterward, he went down to the office, threw the blanket roll on the sofa, then looked out the window.

The crew was just finishing loading their packs on their extra horses. He could see through the back window that Shores had tied his horse inside the barn and unsaddled him.

Then Walt walked back to the file case on the far side of the desk. Here, in essence, was the history and guts of Bar D. Breeding records, sales, purchases, household and ranch expenses, records that Walt had managed until the death of his father; after that, he didn't bother with them. Sam, however, would miss them, and Walt smiled. A faint curiosity made him pull a file drawer and take out a folded map. He tossed it on the desk, where he unfolded it, spread it out, and located Hackberry Creek, which paralleled the county line but was north of it. And Pemberton's place was north of it, which put it in Brewer County. If he got the Pemberton place he would be out of Cable's jurisdiction.

He put the map back in the drawer, then moved over to look out the window. The crew was gone, but to make sure he put on his hat, went outside, and headed for his old house. It was empty and dirty, but the cook had left a steak sandwich on the kitchen table, obviously meant for him. He wolfed part of it down, standing at the table, and then remembered that this would be supper too and stopped eating to save the food.

Afterward, he left the house and headed for the bunkhouse. It too was abandoned. At last he was truly alone. Except for him, Bar D was deserted.

He killed what was left of the afternoon by catching his second horse, then turning out the rest of the horses into the horse pasture.

While it was still light, he went back and finished his sandwich, then went back to the barn, saddled his horse, and tied on his blanket roll. Afterward, he went into the tool room that was part of the barn, found a five-gallon can beside the coal-oil drum, and filled the can by using the drum's spigot. Afterward, he took the can to the office, set it on his desk, then took down a windbreaker from the clothes tree and put it on. Later, he went through the almost-dark house and lit every lamp in every room of both floors and opened a window in each room.

It was dark when he left the house through the office. By the light of a half moon he found his way past his old house and bunkhouse. At the far end of the bunkhouse he hunkered down against the end wall.

Across the flats and far distance he could pick up a pinpoint of light which would be the house lamps of the Schuyler place. From childhood he could remember that the Schuylers rose and went to bed with the chickens. They were the only people who could see what was about to happen and report it but once their lamps were out they'd be asleep.

He rolled a smoke, lit it, and by the time the match flare had washed out of his eyes the lamplight was gone. He smoked down his cigarette, ground it out, then rose and headed for the office. Once there, he picked up the can of coal oil and went up to the second floor. There he methodically drenched rugs and furniture with the oil.

Downstairs, he repeated the process, giving special attention to the office and its files. Then he lighted and tossed two matches into the puddles of coal oil around the files, waited for the flames, then left the house.

After putting back the can in the tool room he went to his horse, took the lead rope of his second horse, and reined in at the barn doorway. He could see flames in most second-story windows and at the office window.

Sam, he thought, had a bonfire to clean up after; a bonfire that left him without a house, without any sort of records, without any sort of inheritance except a small house, a bunkhouse, and outbuildings. He'd have to wait until fall roundup to learn how many cattle he had.

He moved out of the barn now and followed the horse pasture fence for a half mile, then halted and looked back. Flames were licking up the outside of the house through the open windows. Soon the shingles would catch and that would be the beginning of the end of Bar D's Big House. Even if the fire was seen now, there was no way the house could be saved, he thought with pleasure, one last favor to himself.

6

Sistie was at the big iron stove, plate in hand, ready to serve up her father's second helping of hotcakes when the doorbell clanged loudly.

"I'll get it," the sheriff said, rising. "This early it's got to be for me."

He left the table, crossed the kitchen, and went down the hall to the front door. Sistie heard it open and then her father said, "Hello, Les. You're out right early. Come in."

"Yeah, and with nothin' but bad news," Les Beecham said. "Somebody burned down the Big House at Bar D last night."

"No!" Cable exclaimed. "Where was Walt and his crew?"

"Not there. Him and his crew was supposed to be off the place by sundown tonight; left early, I reckon."

"How'd you get the news?"

"Tim Scobie. He's one of the new crew I hired. He was cuttin' through our range, headed for town, when he smelled the smoke. He followed his nose and found it."

"Just the Big House, nothin' else?"

"That's right. Sam's out there now waitin' for you."

Cable nodded. "Had breakfast?"

Les shook his head. "No time, but thanks anyway."

"I'm on my way," the sheriff said. "See you out there."

After letting Les out the sheriff came back to the

kitchen, halted just inside it, and looked at Sistie. "You hear that?"

"Every word! It's shameful! Why would anyone do it, Pa? And who would do it?"

"Some people think Walt was stealin' their beef. Some even think Sam knew about it and collected his share. I reckon it could be anybody with a grudge against the Danas."

Sistie only shook her head in bewilderment. "Had enough breakfast, Pa?"

"More than enough. I'd better get out there."

"Can I go with you in the buggy? It's my day off, remember. I know they'll keep people away until you get your look but if I'm with you they'll pass me and maybe some way I could help."

"Why not?" Cable said after a moment's thought. "You're likely to hear some rough talk, though."

"Nothin' I haven't heard before. You go harness up while I clean up the kitchen and make the beds."

The Cable house was a small frame one on the edge of town with land enough to accommodate a small barn with adjoining corral.

Sistie finished her housework and went out the back door to see her father throw his saddle into the box of the buggy.

As she approached Cable said, "If I have to do some ridin' out there I want my own rig."

Sistie nodded, patted Dooley on the nose, and said, "Let me drive, Pa. It's been a long time." She climbed up to the seat, waited for her father to climb in beside her, unwound the reins from the whip socket, and they drove off.

It was a sunny, warm morning, too early to smell of dust later traffic would stir up. Still, the errand her father was on was depressing. He was used to trouble but somehow this was different and Sistie felt a melancholy she couldn't explain. The last Mrs. Dana, without girl children, had given parties at the Big House for the town's growing girls—with the two Dana boys absenting themselves. The Big House, simply, was the grandest place she had ever known, and now it was gone.

She caught the smell of smoke even before they reached the gate, which, as she had guessed earlier, was guarded by two men. They moved to bar the way but when the sheriff waved lazily they recognized him and moved out of the way. As the buggy passed one man called, "Tie up at the small house, Sheriff."

Cable nodded and reached over and took the reins. Sistie looked at the smoldering heap of rubbish that had been the Big House. Ten feet of brick chimney thrust up through the smoking rubble to mark where the living room had been; at the other end of the wreckage was the sturdy hulk of the iron kitchen range. The rest was gone or going on the ground.

Sam and Les were waiting at the tie rail under the big pine. Les took the reins from the sheriff, saying nothing. Sam came up on Sistie's side of the buggy but before he could speak Sistie said, "Oh, Sam, what foul luck! I loved that house and you did too. I'm so very sorry."

"It's done," Sam said, then added, "Very well done, if I can make a bad joke."

In spite of the levity of his words, his tanned face was tight with repressed anger.

"What can I do to help, Sam? Can't I clean up where you'll live?"

"All done, Sistie, but thanks." He looked at Cable now. "Both of you want a closer look at what's left?"

Sistie nodded as Cable said, "I do, for sure!"

Sam handed down Sistie as Cable climbed down. Les fell in with them and together they headed for the ruins.

"I smell coal-oil smoke," Cable said.

"You sure do," Sam said grimly.

Cable asked, "What do you figure? The fire caught and brought down some lamps that fed it?"

Sam shook his head. "No. I think the fire was started on the second floor. The roof caught from it and went up like tinder. The roof fell into the second floor and under all that weight the second floor caved into the ground floor. It burned last. That's its smoke you're smelling."

They halted by the burned house just to the windward of the thin smoke still rising from the rubble.

"Any tracks that tell you anything?" the sheriff asked.

"Only Walt's. He made a couple of trips to the barn from the office. The tool shed is in the barn and that's where the coal-oil barrel is stored," Sam said. "The crew left without Walt and earlier."

"Why are you sure of that?" Cable asked.

"Walt's horse has feet the size of a banjo. And his tracks were missing when the crew rode out. They headed north and they split quick. No herding their extra horses. The dust might attract some attention."

"What if it did, Sam?" Sistie asked.

"Ride out together, leaving a fire laid in the Big House, whoever saw the herd and the crew would remember," her father said. He looked at Sam. "What you're sayin' is Walt waited alone here till dark, then touched it off."

"That's my guess. No smoke would be seen to give it away. One close neighbor. If the light from the fire woke him, he'd figure it was too late to help. If the crew couldn't handle it, what good was he?"

"Any notion where Walt's headin'?"

"He never said and I didn't ask," Sam replied.

Les spoke for the first time now. "Walt's leased a line camp up Brush Creek. But then that's not your county, is it, Mort?"

Cable flushed. "I only want to talk to him!" he said angrily.

"Then you better check on his tracks," Sam said. "Come on."

Sistie stayed where she was and so did Les, who had already seen the tracks. When Sam and the sheriff were out of earshot, Sistie looked at Les and said, "Pa's mad. What did you mean when you said Brush Creek wasn't in his county, Les?"

"He won't go out of the county, even if he should," Les said bluntly.

"What are you saying?"

"Ask him."

"I will. But now I'm asking you."

Les told her then of the proof he had of Walt's rustling and selling the stolen beef to the agency on forged bills of sale. Her father, he said, refused to investigate because the cattle weren't in his county.

Sistie had listened in rapt silence and now she said, "If that's true, Les, how do you explain Pa?"

"Old man Dana got your Pa elected again and again. He was loyal to the Danas, but you can't be loyal to both sons. One of 'em ain't worth it."

"Walt, you mean. If he set this fire, why did he?"

"Cussedness. If he wouldn't sell, Sam told him he'd put the Cattle Association detectives on him." He tipped his head toward the rubble. "This is just gettin' even."

Sam and her father were heading back toward them now. Sistie pondered what Les had told her. Courthouse gossip had never hinted at what Les had told her of her father. This was man talk, saloon talk, but it had a ring of truth to it.

Sam and her father halted beside them. Cable pulled off his glasses, yanked out his shirt tail, and wiped off the sweat and dust from the lenses, saying, "I'll talk with

Walt, Sam." He put his glasses back on and tucked in his shirt tail.

"Want me along?" Sam asked. "I'm the owner."

"Or me with the new crew?" Les asked.

"No to you, Les. Yes to you, Sam," the sheriff answered. "We'll ride over to Ridgeway tomorrow and pick up Sheriff Munson. After he hears what we have to say, we'll find Walt." He looked at Sam now. "Am I right if I tell Munson that all ranch records were lost in the fire?"

"Except for what Cy Allen holds. Walt hasn't used him for a couple of years," Sam answered. "Yes, you could say all ranch records were burned."

Les picked up sounds, turned, and saw a pair of riders approaching the small house. "The new crew is showing up. I better get over there." He left and now Sam, the sheriff, and Sistie headed back for the buggy. There Sam handed up Sistie, thanked her for the offer of help, and then said to Cable, "I'll see you tomorrow, Mort."

"I'll be early, Sam."

Sam handed him the reins and said, "I'll be waiting."

After the buggy passed the two guards, Sistie said, "So you're going to go after Walt out of our county?"

Cable looked at her and smiled. "You've been talking to Les. Yes, I am. This isn't unprovable rustling; this is plain arson in my county and I'll prove it."

Sistie kept remembering an unsmiling, rather grim-faced Sam. There was little to remember about him, since he was older than she and he had been away from Garrison most of the time since she had grown up. He was handsome and in a way she couldn't explain to herself different from and more worldly than the other men she had known. She supposed without knowing that most young women he had known had found him as strangely attractive as she had this afternoon.

7

Sam and Sheriff Cable rode into Ridgeway in late morning. The county-seat town was wedged in a notch of a pine-covered ridge which had room only for the main street, which held most of the business buildings and was paralleled by a sidestreet on either side of it.

It had been a hot ride and Sam was thirsty and would have liked to suggest a beer but he reckoned that in Sheriff Cable's mind time was of the essence.

The courthouse was a frame two-story corner building; the courthouse on the ground floor and the Masonic rooms on the second. They left their horses at the tie rail and moved onto the covered boardwalk and through the open doors of the ground floor. Cable led the way down the long corridor flanked by county offices identified by a sign with gilded letters on a black background that jutted into the corridor over each office.

The sheriff's office was in the left rear and Cable walked through the doorway, headed for a flat-topped desk in the left rear corner of the room. Behind it and facing the doorway was a stocky, wide-shouldered man whose bald head was fringed with stiff gray hair. He was alone in the office and at the sound of footsteps he looked up, recognized Cable, and came to his feet, smiling out of a square, broad face in need of a shave.

Rounding the desk, he extended his hand and said, "Good to see you, Mort. It's been a hell of a while, hasn't it?"

"Too long, Emil," Cable said pleasantly and they shook hands. Then Cable introduced Sam, saying, "This is Sam Dana, the new owner of the Bar D."

Sam and Munson shook hands and Munson gestured to the two wooden armchairs on either side of the desk. Cable took the chair closest to the sheriff's.

Munson waited until they were seated and then sat down himself.

"What brings you up this way, Mort?" Munson asked.

"Well, I reckon you could say Sam Dana had a little trouble down our way and I think it's moved into your county, Emil." He went on to tell of the fire that had leveled Bar D's Big House. A *set* fire, he was careful to say. Munson listened as Cable described the circumstances of the fire. Everything, he said, pointed to Walt Dana, Sam's half brother, who had sold his share of the ranch to Sam and been told to move himself and his crew out by Tuesday sundown. The fire was set Monday night and razed the Big House. The old crew headed for Brush Creek, for their lease line camp was in Brewer County, Munson's county. He'd come to Munson for help since Brush Creek was not in his own county.

Munson leaned back in his chair, steepling his fingers and looking at Sam. "You figure Walt set the fire?"

"I'd admire to ask him since that's why we're here."

"Well, he's in my county all right, but not on Brush Creek."

"Sure of that, Emil?" Cable asked.

Munson dipped his head in affirmation. "Like they say, I got it from the horse's mouth. Old Pemberton—he owns the Circle P—came into town yesterday afternoon before the bank closed and deposited a big check. Said he'd sold out lock, stock, and barrel to Walt Dana. He got so drunk last night I had to believe him. It's a sorry place and he was lucky to unload it; but that's where we look for Walt Dana."

"Got your county warrant?" Munson asked. "Guess you'll likely need one too from Brewer County. I'll pick it up on the way out."

The three men rose, Munson leading the way, and went down the corridor to the county clerk's office. Before Munson entered he asked to see Cable's warrant, which Cable took out of his hip pocket and gave to him. Munson was only a minute in the clerk's office; then he came out with his warrant and gave Cable back his own.

"My horse is out back. I'll be with you in a minute," Munson said. He retraced the way to his office, passed it, and went out the back door.

Cable and Sam went out the front door and halted in the shade of the boardwalk's wooden awning.

"Didn't take Walt long to find a new kennel, did it?" Cable asked.

"He had to set that up real quick," Sam observed. "Looking ahead, maybe?"

"Well, he had to run somewhere out of my county, but I don't think he run far enough."

When Sheriff Munson rode up the sidestreet and they saw him, they mounted and joined him. They rode down the valley and then headed west toward the far mountains along a dim, dusty wagon track.

On the way to Circle P, Cable and Munson talked about old times while Sam, siding Cable, listened to their conversation but did not really hear it. He was wondering how Walt would receive two sheriffs, each with a warrant for his arrest.

It took them an hour's ride across dry grasslands to come in sight of a lone, small log cabin, a single sod-roofed log barn to the north of it. There were horses in the corral bunched in the shade of a big cottonwood. Since they headed straight for the cabin, Sam guessed this was Walt's brand new Circle P spread.

As they approached it, a man stepped out from the house onto its small porch and was followed by two other men. Riding closer, Sam saw that all three were carrying rifles, almost as if they expected this visit.

As they approached the big cabin, Sheriff Munson moved his horse ahead of Cable's and Sam's, then dismounted just short of the porch.

Sam heard him say to the three men, "Walt Dana owns this place now, I hear. Where can I find him?"

Wiley Shores, Walt's foreman, stepped forward to the top of the two log steps. There was no mistaking the star of the sheriff's office pinned to Munson's shirt nor the similar star displayed on the breast pocket of Cable's shirt.

Shores' broad face was pleasant, his tone almost cordial as he said, "Walt and a couple of the boys rode out the morning. They aim to look over the stock he bought and buy some more."

"Where?" Munson asked.

"I don't know. I don't reckon he knew. He aimed to look over what he bought."

"When do you reckon he'll be back?" Cable asked.

"He never said," Shores said blandly. "All I know is they took blanket rolls and some grub."

"He headed for Brush Creek?" Munson asked.

"Hell no, that's where we come from yesterday."

"Reckon you could find him for me?" Munson persisted.

"I don't know where to look," Shores said. "This country's new to him and me too." He looked at Sam now and his face hardened. "Ain't you Walt's brother?"

"Half brother," Sam corrected.

"What do you want with Walt?"

Sheriff Cable answered, "The Big House at Bar D was burned to the ground Monday night. We'd like to ask Walt about it."

"He don't know any more about it than any of us do." Shores scowled. "What are you trying to say?"

"I just want to talk with him," Cable said.

"About the fire? Hell, he was with us starting at noon till this morning." He glanced at the two crew members. "Ain't that right?"

The tall, sullen-looking puncher, one of the two who had greeted Sam on his arrival at Bar D, said, "I rode with him to Brush Creek, ate supper with him, and slept beside him. What could he know about any fire that we don't know?"

Shores nodded and looked again at Sam. "Like I said, we was all with him. Now I'm talkin' to you, Dana, not the two lawmen. Get the hell off this place now!"

"Easy," Munson said. "You're not the owner."

"I'm the boss when the owner's gone and I got orders to keep Sam Dana off this place. He kicked us off his place and I'm kicking him off ours."

Sam swung out of the saddle and moved past Cable and halted at the foot of the steps. "You're a purple liar, Shores. Walt's here 'cause his big horse is here."

"He lamed up and Walt borrowed mine." He lifted his rifle a few inches and said, "Get off Circle P range."

Sam said coldly, "Both Munson and Cable have search and arrest warrants for Walt. I think he's hiding in the house. The only way you can prove he isn't is to let Sheriff Munson search the place. I'll stay here."

"No, you won't," Shores said. "Get back on your horse and ride off this property."

"That changes my mind," Sam said quietly. "I'll go

along on the search with Munson." He turned and asked Cable, "Have I a right to go along with Munson?"

Cable was looking past Sam and he said flatly, quickly, "Drop on your belly, Sam!"

Sam didn't hesitate. He fell facedown in Cable's direction. As he hit the dirt and rolled to one side he heard the flat, close explosion of a rifle. Cable grunted and lurched back in his saddle, his horse dancing to one side.

Sam rolled over on his back, sat up, and saw the smoke rising from the barrel of Shores' rifle. He drew his gun and, without sighting it, fanned the hammer.

Shores' breath escaped him in a savage grunt; he dropped his rifle and his hands went to his midriff just as Munson, drawing his gun, shouted, "Drop your guns, both of you!"

Sam came to his feet, saw the two other crewmen throw down their rifles, and then he looked over his shoulder at Cable. The sheriff had a hand on his left shoulder, his head bowed down with pain. As Sam started for him he heard Munson's order to the crew: "Get off the porch right now!"

Sam hurried over to Cable, who was still mounted, hand still to his shoulder. As he trotted over to Cable Sam whipped off his neckerchief and then halted beside Cable's horse. Before Sam could speak Cable said, "Just a nick, Sam."

Sam extended the neckerchief, which Cable accepted and pressed against his shoulder which was already staining his shirt with blood.

"That was meant for me, Mort, I'm sorry."

Cable nodded. "Better go see what your shot did."

Sam turned and tramped back toward the porch. Shores had been knocked flat on his back. His boots jutted out over the top step. Munson, hearing Sam's footsteps, said to the two disarmed men, "Stay right there," and then he fell in behind Sam, who was climbing the porch steps. Sam halted on the porch and Munson climbed up beside him. The whole of Shores' shirt front was bloody and now Sam knelt and reached for his arm, lifting it, and felt his right wrist for a pulse. He could find none and looked up at Munson.

"I think I killed him," Sam said. Munson knelt beside him and he, too, felt Shores' wrist for any sign of a pulse. Then he nodded his head. Both men rose and Munson said, "He started it and I reckon that's all that matters." Both men went down the steps and faced the two crewmen. "Give me your names," Munson said.

The sullen, taller man said, "Steve Palmer. What's yours?"

Munson ignored him and looked at the other man.

"Harry Carmichael," the second man said.

"Where's Walt?" Munson asked.

Palmer answered, "Hell, he took off as soon as he seen your dust through the glasses. Don't ask me where to."

"Why'd he run?" Munson prodded.

"I never asked. I only work for him. Him and Shores was out on the porch with the glasses. Shores called in to us to get our rifles and his own. Walt went through the house and out the back door and took my horse because he was saddled and tied out back."

"Show me the house. Lead the way," Munson said to Steve, gesturing to the house with a wave of his gun.

The puncher led the way, skirting Shores' body. Munson followed and Sam trailed him. The unswept living room held a cracked leather sofa, two wooden rocking chairs, and a pile of blanket rolls in front of a square table against the front wall. Straight ahead was a narrow corridor, a curtained bedroom on each side. Munson brushed aside the rotting curtain of each room, had his look, and then went down the corridor to the kitchen, where the puncher was waiting.

As Munson and Sam came into the kitchen and halted, Steve said, "Well, you've seen it."

"Show me the barn, the privy too," Munson said.

Sam had already spotted the kitchen cupboard against the back wall. When the two men went out the back doorway Sam went over to the kitchen cabinet, opened the top doors, and saw what he wanted—a row of jelly glasses on a shelf. He took down two of them, closed the doors, and backed off a step, guessing that the right-hand lower section would hold the flour bin. When he pulled the handle and the triangular bin sloped out he smiled faintly. The bin was half full of flour. He took one of the jelly glasses and dipped it full of flour and closed the bin, then really looked around the kitchen.

On the counter by the sink pump was a half-full bottle of whiskey. Moving over to the sink, he pumped the other glass half full of water, filled the other half with whiskey and, both glasses in his left hand, headed back through the house.

When he opened the front door, his coming raised a swarm of flies from the dead man lying on the porch. Neither Cable and his horse nor the second puncher were where he had left them.

Moving through the swarm of flies, his hand close to his holstered gun, he moved off the porch and went left to the shady side of the house. He saw Cable sitting on the ground in the shade, his gun in his lap, his attention on the distant corral where their horses were being watered by the second puncher.

Cable heard Sam's approach and looked around, then smiled meagerly.

Sam stopped beside him. "Hurtin' some?"

"A little, like a skinned shin."

Sam held out the drink, which Cable accepted, and Sam said. "Leave a dab to wipe off the blood."

Cable, seldom a drinker, swigged thirstily at his drink and almost drained it in three deep gulps.

Afterward Sam helped the sheriff out of his shirt and pulled back his bloodwet underwear to expose the bloody gash on his right shoulder at the base of his neck. The wound began to bleed again and now Sam poured flour from the other glass into the wound and it immediately began to soak up the blood, forming a sort of sterile scab. Cable dampened a corner of the neckerchief with the remaining water and scrubbed the dried blood off his side and belly.

He was buttoning his shirt over his bulky bandage when Munson and the two punchers, one leading Cable's horse, came around the back of the house and halted before him.

"No sign of him," Munson said. He looked at the two punchers. "I didn't see a wagon back there."

"Pemberton took it. Said he'd bring it back."

"That's your problem. I did see a shovel in the barn. You got a dead man on the porch. Better get him underground."

The two punchers looked at each other. Then Palmer said, "Jesus."

Sam said quietly, "Look at the sky."

They all did and saw the half-dozen vultures flying in random lazy circles.

Then Carmichael asked in an aggrieved tone of voice, "Can we pack him to town?"

"If you've got a horse that'll hold still for the load, sure," Munson said. He spoke to Cable now, "You ready, Mort?" At Cable's nod of assent, Munson spoke to the two punchers. "You tell Walt to come to town real quick and see me. If he don't, I'll raise a posse to ride him down real quick."

Sam held out his hand to help Cable up but the sheriff waved him away, rose by himself, and mounted his horse without assistance. They rode off under the circling vultures.

8

Sam didn't waken Cable when he got up, dressed, had breakfast in the hotel dining room, then went out into the street and headed again for the courthouse.

Sheriff Cable had taken some punishment at the hands of the doctor Munson had recommended. Cable's wound was taken more seriously by the doctor than by Cable himself. The doctor had cleaned the wound, put in a dozen stitches to close it, and ordered Cable to carry the arm in a sling in order to keep the weight of his arm from tearing out the stitches. At first the doctor suggested a day in bed, which Cable promptly rejected. The second suggestion was that Cable be returned to Garrison in a buggy; that, too, Cable rejected. The only thing he agreed to was the sling, which was only common sense.

Sam headed for the courthouse and stopped by to see Munson. In answer to Sam's question, Munson had said no, Walt hadn't shown up. If he hadn't shown up by tomorrow Munson was going after him with a posse.

While he was talking with the sheriff his deputy came in and Sam was introduced. Toby Parker was a bantam of a man, perhaps thirty with hair so pale it was almost white and a kind of aggressive friendliness.

Sam asked, "What if Walt shows up on his own, what happens?"

"Toby takes him down to see Mort," Munson said. "Campbell County pays for the trip. I hope it happens that way, so we don't have to hunt him down."

"Then what?" Sam asked.

"No telling. It's a bailable offense. No one was hurt and I guess he'd be walking the streets in short order—on bond, of course."

Sam shook hands with them both, saying, "Thanks for your help, Sheriff. I hope Walt comes in on his own and spares you chasin' him."

Munson smiled wryly. "That makes two of us."

On the boardwalk, Sam headed for the livery stable where he had put up the horses last evening. He was thinking again with slow anger that Walt was his own kind of fool. If he was chased down or even if he gave himself up, there was bound to be a trial. That meant bringing in Walt's lying crew to testify at his trial in Garrison. Cy Allen would have to disqualify himself as judge because he had represented three Dana men. It would be ugly and costly for everyone involved and there was no assurance that Walt wouldn't go free. There were no witnesses to the fire itself except Walt, who would willingly perjure himself on the stand with lying witnesses to back him up. All in all, it was a sorry mess.

At the feed stable he and the hostler caught his own and Cable's horse and saddled up. Sam paid up, mounted, and led Cable's horse back to the hotel. Leaving the two horses at the hotel tie rail, Sam went into the plain but comfortable lobby.

At his entrance Sheriff Cable, arm in canvas sling, came to his feet and Sam went over to him, eyeing him carefully before he glanced at the clock above the desk. It was after ten o'clock, with a slow ride ahead.

"Why didn't you wake me?" Cable asked, and only then said, "Mornin', Sam."

"If you didn't wake up then you needed the sleep, I reckon. Had breakfast?" When Cable nodded, Sam asked, "Hurtin' any?"

"A little. So would you if somebody'd been hem-stitching you."

"How'd you get into the clean shirt?"

"Went out into the hall and whistled in the clerk. He helped me."

Sam nodded and said, "I'll get my blanket roll," and left him. He went down the corridor to their room, where a Mexican woman was making up the beds.

"Buenos días."

Sam smiled and said, *"Buenos días. ¿Como le va?"*

"Poco, poco."

Sam picked up his blanket roll, went out again, waved carelessly, and left the room. Checking with the clerk, he found that Cable had already paid the bill, and he headed for the street where Cable, blanket roll under his arm, was waiting by their horses. He tied the two blanket rolls behind the saddles, and took down both canteens and filled them for the trip from the pipe that emptied into the watering trough which lay at the break in the tie rail. When he had filled the canteens and started back to the horses he saw that Cable had already mounted. After slinging canteens over the saddlehorns, he handed Cable his reins, then mounted himself.

"I said goodbye to Munson for you. Lead off and set your own pace. Just keep those stitches in."

Sam let Cable set his own pace, which was a sensibly slow one. At the crossroads store with a cantina called Llano with scattered adobe houses seemingly built at random, they nooned in the shade of the store porch. After Cable was seated on the porch, Sam went inside the store, bought a sack of crackers and jerky, and then went into the saloon and asked the tall, balding, wry-faced bartender for one pint of whiskey and two glasses of beer. As the bartender drew the beers and reached behind him for the pint of whiskey he said, "You can eat in here if you want, Sam. You're the only customer."

"You weren't watching out the window," Sam said. "I've got Sheriff Cable with me outside and he's sort of stove-up."

"Bad, I hope," the bartender said calmly.

Sam gave him a long, careful look, then said, "I remember you but I've lost the name."

"Hank Austin. You should remember. You had your dad fire me from Bar D."

"I remember you now," Sam said. "You were always lookin' for cows in the closest bar. That why you wound up here?"

"Is there a better reason?" Austin asked dryly. "How's Walt? Ain't seen him for a stretch."

"All right, I hear. I haven't seen him either for a while. He bought himself a new spread up in Brewer County."

"Where he can drink when he wants to and where he wants to," Austin said with open malice.

"Maybe that's why he moved out," Sam said easily. He put a couple of silver dollars on the counter and received his change.

Austin didn't bother to either thank him or to carry out the drinks. Sam picked up the tray, put the sack of food on it, and said, pleasantly enough, "See you around."

"I doubt it," Austin said. "This'll last me for a while."

Sam carried his tray back to the store and went out onto the shady porch. He wondered if he should tell Cable about Austin and he decided it wasn't worth the trouble. He had enough no-goods bothering him, and adding this cipher would accomplish nothing.

That was their midday meal then, more medicinal than nutritive—a drink of whiskey followed by jerky and crackers, washed down with beer. After Sam returned the steins to the saloon and returned to the porch, he found that again Cable had mounted and was waiting for him. His color, Sam noted, was not so pale after the food and drink. Sam put the nearly full pint of whiskey in his saddlebag, mounted, and they rode off together.

It was close to dark when they rode down Garrison's main street and turned off the sidestreet that led to Cable's house. Sistie had heard them coming and when they reined in before the front steps Sistie, noting the sling, asked, "What happened to you, Pa?"

Sam answered, "A little trouble, Sistie. Get his bed ready, will you?" As Sistie went in, Sam dismounted and came around Cable's horse. The sheriff was just dismounting but when his boots hit the ground he staggered a little. Sam caught him, straightened him up, and Cable said, "I'm all right, just stiff is all."

Sam took his good elbow and helped him up the steps. Once on the porch, Cable shook off his hands and said, "Stay for supper, Sam. I'll lie down all right."

Sam let Cable make his own way into the house, across the living room, and into the bedroom beyond where Sistie was waiting.

"Sam's staying for supper. Got any?"

"Are you all right, Pa?" Sistie asked.

"Right as rain, just tired."

Seeing that he was no longer needed, Sam went outside and led both horses to the corral. Offsaddling Cable's horse, he slipped both bits, climbed the outside ladder to the hayloft, and forked down feed. As he pitched out hay, he reflected that this had been a rough ride, a rough and exhausting ride for Cable, and he knew that there would be days of discomfort ahead of him.

Back in the house, he saw Sistie moving in the kitchen and he tramped through the hall, taking off his hat and hanging it on the hall tree as he headed for the kitchen.

Almost there, he met Sistie leaving the kitchen, a tray in her hands. Sam flattened against the wall to let her pass and she said, "Go on in, Sam. I'm takin' Pa some soup. That's all he wants."

Sistie went into the living room on her way to Cable's bedroom and Sam moved into the kitchen. There were two places set at the table against the rear wall and the very smell of the kitchen started Sam's belly churning with hunger. He moved over to the stove, lifted the lid of a cast-iron stew pan, and got a brief look before the lid began to burn his fingers and he dropped it.

From behind him Sistie said, "It's hash and potatoes. Sam. Sound all right?"

"I don't know how it sounds. But I know how it smells. Yes. How do you think your dad looks?"

"Hurt and tired. Sit down, Sam. Let me serve up and then tell me what happened. Pa won't."

They were both served and seated and began to eat. Sam told her what had happened at Circle P and he blamed himself for triggering the trouble. Her father, he said, had saved him from being shot in the back and he caught the bullet intended for him. Sistie interrupted only once and that was to get seconds for Sam.

When Sam had finished his account Sistie said, "You and Pa are lucky to be alive. But what happens now? Will Walt be outlawed?"

"Unless he gives himself up he will."

Sistie shook her head. "This is all coming too fast for me, Sam. Until day before yesterday I didn't know anything about Walt except that I never liked him or his wife. Now he's proven to be a criminal."

"Not *proven* yet, Sistie."

Sistie rose to clear the table and Sam helped her. As he put the dishes in the sink he noticed for the first time that the counter to the right of the sink pump held something covered by dishcloths. Out of curiosity he lifted the corner of the cloth and saw that it covered many loaves of freshly baked bread. Sam glanced at Sistie. "You're baking for the winter. How are you going to keep it?"

Sistie smiled. "You've forgotten," she said.

"What have I forgotten?"

"The town's anniversary at the church. The Army was garrisoned here twenty-five years ago. Saturday night supper on the church lawn."

Sam nodded. "May I escort you to it, Miss Cable?" Sam said in mock formality.

"I'd love you to," Sistie said. "The army is sending a detail up from Fort Griffin. There will be lots of speeches and lots of good food. The food will be better than the speeches."

Sam grinned. "It better be, or I'll leave you sitting alone." He looked around the kitchen. "Where do you keep your dishtowels?"

Sistie shook her head. "No you don't, Sam. I can clean up in two minutes. Every time Pa offers, I tell him nobody in this house sings for his supper. So on your way, Sam, and thanks for helping Pa."

Sam shrugged. "Even steven, thanks for feeding me. I'll pick you up Saturday, at what time?"

"Five o'clock, Sam, and thanks again for helping Pa."

Sistie followed him through the hall, where he picked up his hat and she let him out, bidding him goodnight.

Sistie returned to her father's room. He was sleeping and she turned the lamp down low, picked up his dishes, and returned to the kitchen. As she began to clean up she thought again about Sam. He was a good man, she told herself—kind, knowledgeable, and, at long last, a steady man with property. He would, she thought, make a fine husband and father to the children she wanted.

9

Walt and two of his hands rode into Circle P just after sunup. They reined in at the tramped mound of earth some fifty yards west of the house. The crude board cross at one end of the watered-down earth told its own story.

Walt, his heavy face long unshaven, was scowling as he regarded the grave. Then he looked at his companions and asked, "Who the hell could this be, and why here?"

One puncher shrugged and they heard the back door slam. Looking up, they saw two of the crew approaching them. Walt, missing Wiley Shores, had a swift premonition. The two punchers stopped before them and Walt said, "Wiley?"

At Steve's nod, Walt swore bitterly. He put his horse in motion and headed for the corral, followed by the other crew members.

"Had anything to eat?" Steve called.

"No, and we're hungry," Walt called over his shoulder.

The three of them rode up to the corral gate, off-saddled, and turned their horses into the corral. Walt hurried past the gear he had dropped, heading for the kitchen door. The smaller puncher, Clay Ewing, picked up Walt's saddle and bridle and before he picked up his own he looked at their companion, Fred Beasley, a middle-aged, bent man who on foot was a cripple with a limp but on horseback was a top hand.

"What the hell's happened, Fred?"

The older man said in a surly tone of voice, "Let's go

find out." They took their gear and Walt's to the barn, then headed for the house together.

In the kitchen, Steve was smoking up the room by frying steaks and reheating some fried potatoes. Carmichael was clearing the table and putting clean plates and utensils on the table.

Walt wrenched off his hat, tossed it on a bench, and addressed Steve at the stove, "Who killed him?"

"Sam did," Steve said. He pulled his gloves from his pocket and used one for each skillet as a heat pad. He took both skillets over to the table. Clay and Fred came in then, almost bumping into Steve on their way to the table. As they passed Walt, the skillets smoking, Steve said, "You're in trouble, boss."

Then he said to Harry, "Get the coffee on."

Walt slid down the bench as Steve put the skillets on the rectangular table. Walt helped himself to the meat and potatoes as his riding companions sat down beside him, their hats still on, Steve sat down on the bench opposite Walt while Harry poured coffee into tin cups for them all.

Steve told of the visit yesterday, of Sam and the two sheriffs, of the arguments and of Shores' ordering Sam off the property. Sam's refusal to leave started the shooting. Cable was wounded but Sam had gunned down Shores.

Still talking around a mouthful of steak, Walt said, "You told him I was with you from noon Monday until we came here?"

"We sure did."

"Then what kind of trouble am I in?" Walt demanded.

"You better get into town right now and talk to Munson or he'll have a posse after you for dead sure. He's got a warrant out for you and Cable does too. I reckon he'll turn you over to Cable since the fire happened in Cable's county."

Walt shrugged. "I'll go see Munson and Cable. There's no way Cable can take me if you stick to your story that I was with you. They've got proof of nothing, Steve."

"Don't worry about us backin' your story. You was with us from Bar D to here. But Munson left here madder than hell. If you don't show up real quick, he'll hunt you down real quick, he said. And with his posse."

"That's a bluff," Walt said derisively. "If I'm innocent, why would I come when he whistles?"

"You still don't get it, boss," Steve said patiently. "If he raises a posse, where'll he take it first? Right here. He finds you asleep or whittlin' on the porch, he'll be even madder. So will the posse."

"So what do I do?"

"Soon's you're done eatin', head for town and Munson. Tell him we told you he wanted to see you. Go in alone, like you're aimin' to oblige him."

Walt took a swig of his coffee and asked, "Then what happens?"

"Damned if I know, boss. It's Cable that wants you, because the fire happened in his county. Munson'll likely send you to him."

For the first time since he'd planned the fire, Walt was beginning to regret it. Still, with his crew willing to give him a bulletproof alibi, there wasn't much Sam or Cable could do to pin it on him.

Walt rose, stepped over the bench, and put on his hat. "No way of tellin' how long I'll be gone. Steve, you're the new ramrod."

Steve grinned. "Thanks, boss. If I am, here's my first order." He looked at Carmichael. "Harry, go saddle up the boss's horse, will you?"

Carmichael nodded, put on his hat, and went out. Walt continued, "You and the boys keep away from town till I get back. God knows when that'll be."

"If we can't go into town for a beer or two, is it all right if I go in for a bottle now and then?" Steve asked.

"As long as you're alone, sure."

The door opened and Harry came in and said, "The big boy's saddled, boss."

"You've all got your pay. Give your checks to Steve when he goes in and he'll cash them. Steve, you keep track of what you spend for grub and I'll pay you back. You're making Wiley's pay—fifty-five dollars a month." He scowled. "What have I forgot?"

"We'll make out. Just you make out," Steve said.

Walt went out, the crew following. They watched him mount the big dun, wave carelessly, and head east toward Ridgeway. Back in the cabin, the three men set about cleaning up the kitchen. They were silent for a while until Harry said, "What do we call you now, Steve?"

"Same as always," Steve said.

"You kind of give him a scoldin'," Harry said.

"He's a stubborn man," Steve said mildly. "I had to." *Stubborn,* Steve reflected. *More like muleheaded,* he thought. Surely Cable would make all the trouble he could for Walt over the fire. When the case came up, he didn't doubt that they would be called down to Garrison for Walt's trial. But would there be a trial? he wondered. Right now the cards were stacked against there being one. No witnesses to the fire and a full coverup for Walt. If the crew stuck to their story that Walt was with them from noon Monday until they moved here, there were no grounds for holding Walt. Still and all, Walt had done a damn stupid thing.

Walt remembered where the courthouse was in Ridgeway and he went directly to it. He had not seen a single rider, let alone the dust that a posse would raise. Steve had been right in urging him to get to Ridgeway as soon as possible, he admitted grudgingly to himself. This visit to Munson should get the sheriff off his back.

Dismounting at the tie rail, he went into the courthouse and walked down the corridor, reading the signs. When he was in sight of the rear door he wondered if the courthouse held a basement and then he spotted the overhead sign above the last doorway on his left. Would he know Munson if he saw him? he wondered. He had heard him described as burly and bald and over fifty-five, but he hadn't thought to check that with Steve.

He went into the room and saw two men talking across a flat-topped desk in the left rear corner of the room. The man seated behind it had to be Sheriff Munson because he was both bald and burly. The other man in the chair facing Munson was blond and slight. Walt walked angling across the room and belatedly took off his hat. As he approached the desk he said, "You're Sheriff Munson, I reckon." He stopped and Munson nodded. "I'm Walt Dana. My crew out at Circle P tells me you want to see me."

Munson rose and extended his hand across the desk and unsmilingly both men shook hands, saying the amenities. The other man rose now and Munson said, "This is Toby Parker, my deputy."

Walt and Parker shook hands and Munson gestured to the third chair, saying, "Sit down."

When Walt was seated Munson sat down, as did Parker. Munson said then, "If you've talked with your crew you know pretty much what happened at your place."

"All I know is that you and Sheriff Cable both have warrants for my arrest on a charge of arson at Bar D. No, that's not all I know. My foreman is dead and buried."

"He tried to kill your brother," Munson said bluntly. "Shores ordered him off your property; then, when he didn't leave, Shores tried to kill him. He shot first, Sam ducked, shot back, and killed Shores."

"I know all that," Walt said heavily. "What did I have to do with all that?"

"That's not why I asked you to come in. The warrant says you are wanted for arson in Cable's county."

"That's what the boys said. Did you talk with them?"

Munson nodded. "They all said you were with them from noon Monday until you moved to Circle P."

"That's true," Walt said flatly. "Tell me how I could start a fire at Bar D when I was fifteen miles from it with my crew."

"You'll have a chance to ask that in court. I'm neither judge nor jury. I'm just sendin' you back to Sheriff Cable of Campbell County."

"But this is a damn lie!"

"You'll have a chance to prove it," Munson said coldly. He looked at Parker. "You ready to take off, Toby?"

"Right now," Parker said.

Munson said to Walt, "You ready, Dana?"

"It don't look like I have much choice, does it?"

"That's right," Munson said. "No choice at all."

Walt stood up, hat in hand. "But I think I do. Both you and Cable talked with my crew. They were with me from Monday noon till we moved here. You say Cable says the Big House was burned down. I'll take your word for it because you took his, but I wasn't connected with any fire in any way." He put on his hat. "I'm going back to Circle P, not down to see Cable."

Munson said dryly, "It's your choice. I'll be out at Circle P with a posse around two o'clock. You better be there."

"I want a lawyer. Mine's in Garrison."

"Parker will take you to him, unless you'd rather be escorted down there by a posse."

Walt knew immediately that he'd said too many wrong things to the wrong people in the wrong way; but to accept this wholly and without protest would be a coward's way out. He said then, "I'll go then, but both you and Cable will get hell sued out of you for false arrest." He looked at Parker. "Let's go."

10

Walt and Parker arrived in Garrison in early afternoon and went directly to the sheriff's office in the courthouse. Cable was not in but his deputy, Joe Peterson, booked Walt, took him down to the cell block in the basement and locked him in a cell with Toby Parker watching.

When his bedroll was examined for concealed weapons Walt said, "I want to see my lawyer, Howard Olsen."

"I'll see him after we close, Walt. We're shorthanded today. Sorry about that." Peterson was a tall and chubby young man who, like his boss, wore steel-rimmed glasses. It was obvious that he didn't like Walt in that he really wasn't a bit sorry that he could not accommodate him at the moment.

"I've got a right to see my lawyer right now!"

Parker said quietly, "I'll find him and tell him you're here, Dana. Where do I go?"

"Come on forward and I'll tell you," Peterson said.

Walt was already pacing the cell block and he didn't bother to thank Parker. Neither did Parker bother to say goodbye. Some ten minutes later, Peterson appeared with Olsen, let him into Walt's cell, and locked it behind him, saying, "Bang that dipper on the bars. I'll hear it." Then he left.

Howard Olsen, dressed in a dark townsman's suit, shook hands with Walt and seated himself at the foot of the cot. He was a tall, cadaverous-looking man of forty-odd years with a gaunt, hollow-cheeked face that reflected a cheerful cynicism. He said then, "Tell me about it, Walt."

Walt did just that. He told of his witnesses who would swear that they had been with him since Monday noon and provided an unbreakable alibi. He was not guilty of the arson at Bar D and couldn't guess who was. Olsen got the names of the old Bar D crew, wrote them down in a pocket notebook, and then listened to Walt's account of the shooting and killing of Wiley Shores in his absence.

Olsen asked a few questions and then rose. "I'll go see Cy Allen now. If it comes to a trial, which I doubt, he'll have to disqualify himself because of the multiple conflict of interest. There'll be a preliminary hearing tomorrow mornin' and I'm sure you'll be freed on bond." He put his notebook back in his coat pocket and said, "This is a wild one, Walt, but I think you'll be out by noon tomorrow. I'll bang the dipper and let me get out of here."

Les Beecham returned to Bar D from Garrison with a load of supplies in a borrowed wagon. The news in town, he told Sam, was that Walt had been brought down from Ridgeway by a deputy sheriff, locked up in the Campbell County jail, and was scheduled for a preliminary hearing before Cy Allen first thing tomorrow morning.

Sam and the crew had spent the day going through the rubble of the fire and loading wagon after wagon of debris and dumping it in a dry arroyo east of the ranch buildings. All of them except for Les were dirty, tired, and hungry when the clang of the triangle announced supper. After they had eaten, Sam drew Les outside into the dusk and headed for the barn while the rest of the crew tramped out into the evening, heading for the bunkhouse. At the barn Les and Sam hunkered down on their heels, backs against the weathered boards.

"How's Cable?" Sam asked.

"I stopped by Sistie's office. She said he skipped work today. He was hurtin' some."

"He'll be at the hearing, won't he?" Sam asked.

"Sistie said he would be, for sure."

"I think I'd better see Cy after the hearing tomorrow," Sam said.

"Walt can't leave the county until the trial date is set, can he?"

"I don't think so, but I'm no lawyer, Sam. They may turn him loose. No one saw him set the fire, so there's nary a witness."

When County Judge Cy Allen stepped into his waiting room he found Sam Dana and a man he scarcely knew seated and talking idly. Both men rose at his entrance and Cy said, "Mornin', gentlemen. You both beat me to work." Without waiting for a response, he continued, "Glad you could make it, Sam." To the other man he said, "Harvey, Sam's first on my appointment list."

He walked to his office door, unlocked it, stood aside, and said, "Come in, Sam."

When both men were seated behind the closed door at Cy's desk, Sam asked, "How did the hearing go, Cy?"

"Terrible, to put it bluntly," Cy said. "Walt pled innocent to the charge of arson. He said he was with his crew from Friday until yesterday. Cable testified that the two crew members verified this. I let Walt free under a five-hundred-dollar bond and confined him to Campbell County."

"Did you set a trial date?"

Cy grimaced. "No, I didn't. I don't think there'll be a trial, Sam. If Walt and his men stick together on their stories, Walt couldn't have set the fire."

"I think he did and so does Mort. How do we prove it?"

"With perjuring witnesses, you don't," Cy said wryly.

"Why are you confining Walt to Campbell County if you don't think there'll be a trial?"

"For other reasons," Cy said bluntly. "Walt's got a wife here who is damn close to starving. Walt doesn't give her any money and she earns maybe a dollar a day clerking at Safford's Dry Goods. Walt gives her no support money because she won't divorce him or let him divorce her."

"I don't follow you, Cy. What's that got to do with keeping Walt in Campbell County?"

"Plenty, if you'll help. I'm disqualifying myself in Walt's case as of now. As county judge I'm allowed to preside over the preliminary hearings, but if the case goes to my court I will have to disqualify myself. I've represented too many Danas, a father and two sons. I can't help but be biased and I'll tell the district attorney just that. A prejudiced judge has no business hearing this case, and I'm prejudiced. Instead, I intend to represent Rita Dana, if you could persuade her to file suit against Walt for nonsupport. Can you?"

"So that's it."

"Exactly. This is professional ethics. I can't go to her and ask her to hire me even if I won't charge a fee. But you could, Sam."

"Where will we meet without giving it away?" Sam asked.

"You're talking with me now and I'm telling you I'm disqualifying myself. Since I told you that, there's no reason why you shouldn't bring a client to meet with me at my house tonight."

"You sure you're clear on this, Cy?"

"I disqualified myself before the district attorney. I'm still a lawyer, still willing to accept clients who are not involved in this case. Rita isn't. This is a domestic affair even if it does involve Walt."

"Is seven-thirty a good hour for you, Cy?" At Cy's nod, Sam said, "If she'll come, she'll be there by then."

Sam rose now, saying, "I'll see you tonight, Cy."

After the hearing, Walt, Olsen beside him, wrote out a check for five hundred dollars bond money in the sheriff's office and gave it to Peterson, who in turn gave him a receipt. Although Sheriff Cable had testified at the hearing, he had left after his testimony was given. Walt was grateful that he didn't have to face Cable in a postmortem of the hearing.

He and Olsen left the courthouse together and walked as far as Olsen's office beyond the hotel. Walt didn't go in but they shook hands as Olsen went into his ground-floor office. Most of the buildings on the street were two-storied with covered stairways leading to the second floors, and Olsen's was no exception. Walt turned back up the street, headed for the hotel bar, and then realized that he was alone and therefore vulnerable. He halted. It was the first time in months that he had been alone, and a slow panic mounted in him. He had to get off the street and out of sight. Main Street was almost empty but the noon hour was approaching and he knew the hotel saloon would be filling up with the noon drinkers and diners.

He halted just outside the bat wing doors, looking up and down the street, and then went into the barroom. Save for the two bartenders and the houseman, the room was empty. He went to the stool at the bend in the bar and ordered a whiskey and a beer from a taciturn bartender. Walt knew he was recognized and disdained after his beating at the hands of Les Beecham. He paid, drank down a shot of whiskey, and cooled off its fire with a cold beer. He was, he knew, in a tight bind, with no crew to alert him to danger. The word would already be out that the judge had confined him to Campbell County and that he was alone. He was shrewd enough to realize that he couldn't be in the streets after dark. Olsen had promised to send a messenger up to Circle P, asking for two of his crew to come down to join him. What to do in the meantime? he wondered.

Then he thought of Rita. He knew she had a room in a seedy rooming and boarding house and worked as a clerk in the dress goods side of Safford's Dry Goods Store.

He left the bar, walked through the empty dining room and into the busy kitchen, and out the back door and into an alley. He tramped for two blocks, then turned right and picked up the big old house immediately. It was a few houses from the edge of town and in its uncared-for front lawn a paint-flaked sign proclaimed ROOM AND BOARD.

He went up the brick walk, climbed to the porch, and saw the printed sign on the door: WELCOME, RING AND COME IN. Walt gave the bell handle a twist, heard the clang inside, palmed the doorknob, and stepped into a roomy hallway with a parlor on the right and dining room on the left. Three men were seated at the big oval table, being served by a gray-haired old man unabashedly wearing a woman's gingham apron. He was placing bowls of steaming vegetables by platters of meat already on the table.

He had heard Walt's ring and, wiping his hands on his apron, came over to Walt, who asked him, "You serve a hungry man for only one meal, Dad?"

"Sure. One meal or fifty. Same difference." The old boy gestured to three small tables against the hall wall which seated two diners apiece. "The big table is for the regulars. You fly-by-nights gotta sit at the small tables. Take your choice."

Walt went into the dining room and followed him back almost to the kitchen. There he took a chair facing the kitchen door and sat down. After he was seated, more regular boarders began coming into the dining room. He wondered if Rita would recognize his back and come over and say hello. He doubted it. They'd been too long apart and she wouldn't be looking for him.

The old man served him a huge, hot helping of everything and then returned to the kitchen and returned with platters of meat and bowls of steaming vegetables to the big table. As the number of women at the big table increased and the room's quiet dissolved, he could make out the high-pitched chatter of several women, something he'd grown unaccustomed to. He failed to pick up Rita's voice in the women's talk.

The old man stopped beside him and said, "You'll want seconds, won't you?"

Walt had had a long ride and was still hungry and he said, "Sure. It's good food. What do I owe you?" The old man told him and Walt put the coins on the table. The old man thanked him and left for the kitchen again, returning with his refilled plate.

When he had finished he looked behind his back and over his shoulder at the big table. He spotted Rita immediately in the center of the big table, her back to him. Now he left his chair, shoved his coffee across the table, and sat down in the chair facing the room. There was little chance that Rita would notice the shift. He studied her straight, slim back and noticed that she was leaning back in her chair as if finished eating. It took some patient waiting before he saw her rise, say something to an older woman across the table, shove back her chair, and head for the end of the oval table on her way out. He supposed that she was headed for the stairway of the wide hall that led up to the second floor. He got up, followed her, and as she moved toward the stairs he called gruffly, "Remember me, Mrs. Dana?"

Rita halted in her tracks and turned. She was a short, slim, full-bosomed woman in her early thirties with dark hair and almost black eyes over a short, straight nose and full and generous mouth. Her face was thinner than he remembered and her eyes held no warmth at all.

"Yes, way back; way, way, back," she said coldly.

"Can we talk in your room?" Walt asked.

"No men above the first floor," Rita said flatly. She tipped her head toward the parlor, which was filling up with the boarders leaving the dining room, and asked, "Will that do?"

"No," Walt said bluntly. "This is private."

Rita moved past him toward the door, opened it, and looked to her right. Then she turned and said, "Let's try out here."

She went out and Walt followed her. There was a porch swing at the end of the big porch and it was empty. Rita moved ahead of him, her taut haunches swinging enough to move the hem of her skirt from side to side. At the swing she turned and sat down at the street corner of it and folded her arms across the red-flowered shirtwaist. She bent her left leg and put her knee on the seat of the swing, plainly fending off any close contact. There was no invitational pat on the swing seat to invite him to sit next to her.

Walt sat down on the opposite corner, swung up a leg, put a hand on the back of the swing, and said savagely, "Think we can hear each other?"

"Just say what you came to say," Rita said.

"I'm in trouble," Walt said.

"And I'm out of trouble, thank God. Why come to me with it?"

"This mornin' at the arson hearing Judge Allen confined me to Campbell County. I—"

"I know all that. It's all over town."

"I've got to find a safe place to stay until my men get down here. What about right here?"

"Oh no you don't," Rita said coldly. "I don't want you here. If the Pettys do, then I leave. Just like I left before."

"You're still my wife and you'll damn well do what I tell you to," Walt said roughly.

"Try me and see. If you move in here, I move out. But first I go to the sheriff and tell him you're annoying me." Rita shook her head firmly. "It won't work, Walt. I left you because I couldn't live with you."

"Then why in hell won't you divorce me?" Walt said angrily.

"We were married in the church and that means for good. No new wife for you. No new husband for me. We're *married.*"

"Till death do us part," Walt said savagely. "Maybe death will."

"Sheriff Cable would love to hear that," Rita said, unafraid. "If you're looking for a safe place to hide, maybe he'll find one for you in jail, after that threat."

"You're scared to tell him," Walt said.

"I'm not scared of anything. You included," Rita said. "I just don't want to be around you or want you around me. I'm doing all right, you're not. But don't you cry on my shoulder."

Now Rita stood up, straightened her skirt, and said, "Stay away from me for good, Walt."

She left him on the porch, went inside, climbed to her tiny room in the rear, closed the door, then lay down on the bed in her working dress. In less than a minute Rita Lopez Dana was deep in a sleep of exhaustion.

* * *

During his noon meal in the dining room of Garrison House, Howard Olsen came into the dining room alone, spotted Sam immediately, and came over to his table.

Sam rose and they shook hands. Sam said, "You look as lonesome as I do, Howard. Join me, will you? Like a drink?"

"I'd like to, but I've got a date with the judge, Sam. Some private business that would bore hell out of you." He looked over at the door in time to see Cy Allen step into the dining room and look around. Olsen waved to him, said, "See you around, Sam," and moved to join Cy. Sam guessed, without really knowing, that Olsen would make his plea for dismissal of the case against Walt for lack of sufficient evidence.

Finished with his solitary meal, Sam paid at the cashier's desk by the door and headed out to the street. Sistie would be home cooking dinner for her father, and since Sam already had the news that Cable had testified earlier in the morning, his arm still in the sling, there was nothing he had to say to either of them except hello and goodbye.

He did some unimportant shopping until the bank clock told him it was close to half-past one. He headed down the street in the brassy noonday heat and turned in at Safford's Dry Goods. There he bought a pair of heavy work gloves and then moved into the dress goods side of the building and saw Rita moving bolts of dress goods over to the shelves from a freight cart. For a moment he watched her at work. She was thinner than he remembered from last year, and when he moved up to the counter and halted she turned to look at him. Immediately a smile came to her dark face and she extended her hand.

Sam shook hands with her and said, "Do I have to wear a dress to sit down here?"

Rita laughed, "No, Sam. It's good to see you. You look like always, almost too healthy."

Sam sat down on one of the counter chairs, pushed his hat back, and lied sincerely, "You're lookin' fine, Rita, but thinner. They workin' you too hard here?"

"Not too hard, just like everybody else in a town."

She asked about Bar D and they discussed in a neutral way the misfortune of the fire. Rita, of course, had heard the gossip about the morning's hearing, but neither of them brought up the subject. Sam racked his brain for an easy way to introduce what he had to say and could not come up with anything sensible for this time and place. So he asked almost bluntly, "What do you do after work?"

Rita shrugged slightly. "What everybody does, I guess. Go home and eat supper."

"After that?" Sam prodded.

"Why, what everyone else does, I guess. Read or sew a while and go to bed."

"Not tonight you won't," Sam said. "Had a buggy ride lately?" Rita shook her head and Sam said, "What time do you finish supper?"

"Around six-thirty."

"I'll stop by. Let's give you a look at something besides dusty streets and buildings. How does it sound?"

"Like fun, Sam."

Sam rose. "I've got a lot to tell you, Rita, but this is no place for talk. I'll be around at six-thirty. See you then." He gave her a half wave, smiled, and went out into the street, headed toward the livery stable. He swore under his breath. Cy Allen hadn't exaggerated. Rita needed somebody's help and she would never get it from Walt. He had no notion of how to alter Rita's situation if she didn't want to change, but he was sure she did. Maybe on the ride he could get her in a mood to decide. If he couldn't, it wouldn't be for lack of trying.

When Sam reined up the horse and buggy at the stepping block in front of Petty's Boarding House, Rita rose from the porch swing and started down the steps as Sam met her midway to the stepping block. She was wearing the same clothes she'd worn that afternoon but she had a red cardigan sweater thrown over her shoulders.

"Just enough sun left, Sam, and no wind. It'll be nice."

Sam nodded, helped her up the stepping block and into the buggy, then circled the buggy, sat down beside her, and put the horses in motion.

After they had used up small talk Sam said, "I hear Walt's in some trouble over the fire at Bar D."

"He'll get out of it. He always does," Rita said. She went on to tell him of Walt's visit to her that noon, of his plan to hide out at Petty's Boarding House and of her refusal to allow it and of his not-so-veiled threats of reprisal. Her counterthreat to report her conversation with Walt to Sheriff Cable she told in a matter-of-fact tone of voice that made Sam look at her carefully. They were on the outskirts of town now, headed across the flats on a well-traveled, dusty ranch road.

"You're coming close to the real reason I wanted to talk to you alone tonight, Rita."

"Walt, you mean?"

Sam nodded. "Let me talk for a while, will you?" At her nod Sam went on, "You're some crazy, Rita, to put up with what you have. You aren't starvin' but you're shakin' hands with a pretty poor life. I know how you feel about divorce and I can respect it. Still, you have rights in this state, lady, but maybe you don't know it." He looked at her and saw she was alert and attentive. He said then, "Walt isn't supporting you, you're supporting yourself—and damn poorly, I'd guess."

"The best I know how."

"Then take him to court, Rita, for nonsupport. You're his legal wife and in this state even if you're separated from him you're entitled to half of the money he makes."

"Half?" she asked. "But I don't know how much money he makes."

"I know what he made last week because I paid him fifteen thousand dollars for his share of Bar D."

Rita shook her head. "I won't do that, Sam. It was half his before I married him. The money belongs to him."

"You belong to him, too, and the law says you're entitled to support. He could set you up in a place of your own with money to live on, buy you a sewing machine and clothes. Lord, you were wearing that dress when I saw you last two years ago."

"I don't earn money enough to buy a new one or to buy a sewing machine to make a new one."

"Damn it, that's the point!" Sam said brusquely. "You left him because you couldn't live with him. But you're still his wife and the law says he has to support you. Get a lawyer and take it to court."

"What lawyer?"

"Why, Cy Allen, who else?"

"I thought Cy Allen was a judge."

"He is, but he's a lawyer too. This won't go into court, Rita, so he can represent you. This will be an argument between Cy and Howard Olsen. Cy will ask that Walt give you support. If Walt won't, Cy will sue him in your behalf. He'll win, too."

Rita sighed. "I don't know anything about these things, Sam."

Reining in, Sam said, "I do. Let's go back and talk with Cy right now."

11

In early morning a stranger rode into Bar D. Seeing the men starting work, loading rubble from the burning into wagons around the sprawl of ash dust, he rode over to where they were working. Of one of the crew he asked for Sam, and when he was told that Sam had ridden out he asked for the man in charge. The crewman whistled shrilly and when Les looked up he waved him over.

As Les approached the messenger dismounted and when Les came up he recognized him and smiled.

"Hi, Boyce. You're damn near in Injun country for you."

Boyce was a small, wiry, middle-aged man who smiled around a set of tobacco-stained false teeth. They shook hands and Boyce Turner said, "Yeah, that's why lawyer Olsen said to come here. I'm lookin' for Circle P up in Brewer County. Don't know where it's at and thought maybe you could tell me."

"That the spread Walt Dana bought?" At Turner's nod, Les said, "Hell, Walt's due in court this mornin'. Whyn't you ask him?"

"I left before court opened. Olsen told me last night."

"What's Olsen want at Circle P?"

"A couple of witnesses, I reckon. Names are Palmer and Carmichael. Know 'em?"

"Only by their smell," Les said contemptuously. "They'll claim Walt was with them from Friday till they moved to Circle P."

"I wouldn't know," Turner said. "Olsen said just ask 'em to come to Garrison quick and get in touch with him. No warrants, nothing like that. Just the message."

Les felt a small stirring of anticipation as he asked, "You gonna make it there and back today?"

"Olsen said I could. But if he don't know where it is, I don't see how he knows."

"I know a man that can show you." He nodded toward the big pine and said, "Get over in the shade while your man saddles up."

Les saw him start walking his horse toward the shade of the pine and then he went over to the crew. He headed for one man, Bert Downing, whom he was certain knew the country north of here. Les talked with him for only a moment, giving him careful instructions as to the return route, and told him to saddle up and meet him at the pine, and then headed for it himself. When a few minutes later Downing rode up, Turner met his guide and shook hands with him and then mounted. Turner said, "Much obliged, Les. We'll see you around," and the two men rode off.

Les watched them go, headed north, and he wondered if he was planning to make a damn fool of himself. In Sam's absence, leaving no instructions, it was pretty much his own choice. It was obvious that Olsen had told Walt to stay around Garrison until witnesses to his alibi could be brought to town and questioned. If that wasn't so and Walt was free to move, why hadn't he ridden back to Circle P himself? Les's hunch was that Walt needed Carmichael and Palmer not only as witnesses but as protection in the town that considered him a rustler.

Les went back to the crew and began working with them. Like the others, he pulled up his neckerchief over nose and mouth against the choking haze of dust and ashes. When the noon break came Les washed at the bunkhouse pump and went in to eat with the rest of the crew. When they had finished eating and were lighting up their after-dinner smokes, Les hammered on the table with the handle of his knife, which brought immediate silence.

Then he told them what he had planned.

Just before two o'clock Les whistled the agreed-upon signal. When the crew, who had saddled up during the noon break, threw their tools in an empty wagon and headed for their horses, as did Les, the seven men including Les rode out singly so as not to raise a heavy cloud of dust that might be noticed. A half hour later they rendezvoused on the timbered ridge where Les scattered his men among the dense piñon and cedar close to the road that Turner, Downing, and the two witnesses would be traveling. Les himself tied his horse to a cedar close to the road and sat on a rock overlooking and close to the pass road.

Some twenty minutes later he heard the sound of approaching horses trudging up into the pass from the north. He picked up his rifle and slid down the bank to the road.

Turner and his Bar D guide were riding side by side ahead of Palmer and Carmichael, who, Les noted, were heavily armed.

Les moved out into the road and lazily waved to Turner, who reined in, a look of surprise on his face.

"I see you got your witnesses, Boyce. You done your job, so ride on home. I'll see they get in town to Walt."

"But Olsen said I should bring 'em to him."

"I'll do that, Boyce. Good seeing you."

"No witnesses no pay," Turner protested.

"What I'm trying to say, Boyce, is move on. This could be trouble that don't belong to you. You'll get paid. Now move!"

Les slapped the rump of Turner's horse as he headed for Palmer and Carmichael. Both the witnesses had their hands close to their guns.

Les halted and Palmer said, "What the hell is this?"

"Look behind you," Les said.

"You look, Harry. I'm watchin' him," Palmer said. Carmichael turned on his saddle and saw two riders approaching him.

Carmichael turned now and said, "Two behind us."

"You're the looker, Harry. Look head of you." Both men looked past Les and saw two riders approaching and passing Turner. They looked at each other.

"Like I said, what the hell is this, anyway?" Steve said.

"A change of plans," Les said. He called to Downing, "Put a gun on them, Bert." Then he said to both Circle P men, "Just unload your hardware onto the road. Real easy."

Carmichael shrugged and was the first to move. Slowly he lifted his six-gun from its holster, dropped it on the road, and then with equal slowness slipped out his rifle from the saddle scabbard and dropped it. Then he looked at Palmer. "It's your fight now, Steve. Count me out."

Then Palmer disarmed himself and threw his gun and rifle into the road.

"Just tell these fellows behind you where you're going. It's Bar D," Les said. "They'll bring your guns."

On the road back to Bar D they made better time than they had made coming. His crew rode in pairs on both sides of their reluctant guests with Les leading the way, while the man who had picked up the discarded arms brought up the rear.

At Bar D, Les told Carmichael and Palmer to dismount at the tie rail near the big pine and then told the man who had picked up the discarded guns to put them in the barn. The rest of the crew headed for the corral to put up their horses, taking Carmichael's and Palmer's horses with them.

Both Carmichael and Palmer stood silently regarding the ruins of the Big House. Les dismounted, taking his rifle from the scabbard, and said, "Go get a close look."

"I can see what happened," Steve said in a surly tone of voice. "You bring us here to look at it?"

"Partly," Les said.

"What's that mean?" Steve asked.

"Why, you're gonna help clean it up."

Carmichael turned his head to look at Les and said angrily, "We wasn't even here when that fire started! We was fifteen miles away at the Brush Creek line camp!"

Now Steve turned to face Les. "The Big House was standin' like always when we rode out of here."

"With Walt?" Les asked mildly.

"Why, hell yes," Steve said. "He was with us at Brush Creek until we moved to Circle P."

"That fire was set at night," Les said. "Any one of you could have come back after dark and touched it off."

Carmichael asked brusquely, "Why you so sure it was after dark?"

"In daylight the smoke could have been seen in town. Half the town and the pump cart would have been out here helpin' to put it out."

"Anybody with a grudge against Sam could have done it or any kids with matches in an empty house." Carmichael shook his head. "Me, I'm gettin' my horse and ridin' out of here."

He turned and took a couple of steps toward the barn when Les said, "Which leg would you rather have shot from under you?"

Carmichael halted, turned, and said, "All right, but Cable's gonna hear 'bout this. Expect him."

Les saw the crew driving their wagons out of the barn

toward the rubble and then said, "Both of you, start loadin'."

"Damned if I'm workin' for you or for Sam," Palmer said.

"Let's make it you're workin' for me," Les said. "You've run off enough of Diamond B cattle and sold 'em over the mountains to have tolled up a bill. Now start workin' it off!"

"This ain't Diamond B!" Palmer said roughly. "You figure you got a case, take it to court and prove it."

"This is court," Les said flatly. "Get to work."

Carmichael and Palmer exchanged glances and Palmer shrugged, then headed for the pile of ashy rubble, Carmichael following him.

"Don't grab for anybody's gun," Les said. "If they don't shoot you, I will." Neither answered. Now Les tramped back to the shade of the big pine, sat down, and with his back to it put his hat on the ground and his rifle across his legs. Sam, he reckoned, might question the propriety and legality of what he had done, but he'd accept that responsibility even if Sam fired him. This was too good a chance to pass up.

All through the afternoon he watched Carmichael and Palmer. They were, he noted with satisfaction, just as filthy and disgusted as the crew. When he heard a single clang on the bunkhouse triangle, which was only a warning to wash up, he rose and headed for the bunkhouse. He fell in behind Carmichael and Palmer, who dropped in behind the crew, headed for the bunkhouse pump.

It was Palmer who stopped, waited for him, and when Les halted said, "That satisfy you?"

"A little," Les said. "Another day might."

"You keepin' us over until tomorrow?" Carmichael asked angrily.

"You're too right," Les answered.

Les was just finishing washing up when the triangle clanged loudly and the crew filed into the cook-shack door and took their seats on benches lining both sides of the long table. None of the crew talked with Palmer or Carmichael, although they did pass the food platters to them.

The meal finished and the crew split up; some went to the bunkhouse, others sat on the benches flanking the bunkhouse door and watching what seemed to be a ritual game of horseshoes.

Steve came over to Les, who was seated watching the game, and asked, "All right if we get our blanket rolls?"

"If I'm watchin', yes. Let's go."

They headed for the corral and Les watched them catch their horses, offsaddle, and pick up their blanket rolls.

Apparently by agreement, Carmichael left the corral first and headed for the bunkhouse alone. Palmer came out later, blanket roll over his shoulder, and fell in beside Les, heading for the bunkhouse.

"When you expectin' Sam?" he asked.

"Don't know. Why?"

"I wanna talk to him, private," Steve said.

"When he comes in I'll tell him." Behind them a couple of hands were going in through the barn to fork down hay for the horses and graining them at the trough in the small food stall.

"Think Sam'll see me tonight?" Steve asked.

"Don't know why not, but it's up to him."

"I'll be in the bunkhouse," Steve said.

"You damn sure will," Les said, and then left him, headed for the little house.

After leaving Rita at Cy's door and the horse and buggy tied to the hitching post, Sam headed back toward the livery stable. There in the gathering dusk he picked up his horse and headed out for Bar D. On his way he reviewed their conversation and he was still surprised how amenable Rita had been to the suggestion that Cy would only repeat. If between Cy and himself Rita could be persuaded to file suit against Walt for nonsupport, there was no doubt that Cy could win her support money. He himself was some ashamed that he had neglected checking on Rita this past week. These last few days had been busy ones, calling for big decisions, but that really was no excuse for neglecting her when she was so obviously in need of the family's help. Like with everybody Walt had ever had any sort of dealings with, he wanted to dominate them; and he had succeeded only too well with Rita. That, Sam thought grimly, was over for good.

As he rode past the little house, headed for the corral, one of the hands saw him, ran out, and waved him down. When Sam reined in, the man said, "Go get supper, boss. I'll take care of him."

"Much obliged, Barney," Sam said, stepping out of the saddle.

In the near-dark he headed for the door of the lamp-lit cook shack. Apparently the cook had seen his approach and was coming through the kitchen door with his supper at a place already set.

Putting down his plate, the cook said, "You're late, boss, but Les guessed you'd be here sometime."

Sam sat down and began to eat when Les walked in through the kitchen door, a cup of coffee in his hand.

"Far as I could see, you really worked the boys today," Sam said.

"Oh, we had some extra help," Les explained. He went on to tell of his own decision to intercept Carmichael and Palmer and bring them back here and put them to work under his gun. He finished by saying, "Steve Palmer didn't like it much. He wants to see you private when you're through supper."

Sam paused in his eating long enough to say, "I can think of a lot of people I'd rather talk to now. But take him over to the little house. I'll be over when I'm through." He smiled at Les. "Gettin' a little bit even, huh?"

Les grinned. "Well, you wasn't here to say no. I'm not even yet. I'll work 'em both tomorrow if you say it's all right."

Sam nodded and while Les drank his coffee Sam told him what had happened at the hearing, that the whole town knew twenty minutes after it was over. Walt had claimed that four men could give him a foolproof alibi that probably explained Turner's early visit to locate Palmer and Carmichael.

Les rose and said, "I'll go get Palmer."

"Why not both of 'em?"

"He said private, I said yes." He shrugged and went out.

Finished with his supper, Sam rose, took off his gun and shellbelt, picked up his hat off the bench, put his gun on the bench, and went out the cook-shack door, heading for the lamp-lit little house. He entered through the side door that opened on the living room, which had been converted into the Bar D office. Les sat in the straight chair whose back was to a desk that was the converted dining-room table; facing him and seated on the sofa was the tall, sullen-faced puncher who, along with Shores, had greeted him on the first morning of his return.

At Sam's entrance both men stood up.

Steve said, "Howdy, Mr. Dana. Name's Steve Palmer."

Sam only nodded and tossed his hat onto the desk.

Palmer said to Les, "You said private."

"It will be, but I'll be outside. Don't forget it." He walked toward the front door of the living room, went out, and closed it behind him.

Sam moved over to Les's vacated chair, sat down, and said, "What's on your mind, Palmer?"

Steve ran both hands in the hip pockets of his Levis and slowly started to pace the length of the room, head down. To Sam he was pretending to rehearse a decision at which he already had arrived. Halting in the middle of the room, Palmer said, "Didn't much like the way I was brought here by your foreman."

"You weren't supposed to," Sam said coldly. "He brought you here for a reason."

"Me and my partner was on our way to talk to the district attorney. Then your crew jumped us and brought us here."

"Start over," Sam said coldly. "Walt's lawyer, Olsen, sent a man to bring you in."

"So you know why."

"All of Garrison does. You and Carmichael and two of your crew are going to give Walt an alibi on that arson charge. You're going to claim he was with you. So will the other two."

"You're a hell of a mind-reader, Dana. How do you know what I was going to tell?"

"Anything but the truth, I reckon."

"But what if I did tell the truth?" Palmer said. He moved a couple of steps toward Sam and halted. "Would it be worth anything to you?"

"Put it plainer," Sam said.

"What if I told Cable and the district attorney that Walt wasn't with us when he said he was?"

"I didn't mean that," Sam said. "You asked what it was worth to me if you said that."

"Well, what *is* it worth? In money, I mean."

"I'll tell you what it's worth to both of us—a jail sentence apiece," Sam answered dryly.

Palmer scowled. "How do you figure that? I'll be tellin' the truth."

"Four men, counting Walt, will swear you're lyin'. You'll also be charged with soliciting a bribe."

"What's that mean?"

"Asking me for money to say Walt wasn't with you. If I paid you any money I could be charged with bribery." Sam shook his head. "It was a coony try, Palmer, but it won't work. No money."

Palmer reflected only briefly, then grinned. "Who heard me ask you for money? Nobody. No witnesses, my word against yours."

The front door opened and Les stepped into the room, then said, "He's got a witness, me. I heard it all."

Palmer wheeled, looked at Les, and said, "You lied, damn you! I said private, and you said yes!"

Les walked slowly toward him and said coldly, "I said I'd be outside. I was outside. You just didn't notice the front window was open."

Palmer looked beyond him and saw the window that Les had opened before he brought him here.

"You lied, I say!"

Les tossed his rifle on the sofa and said, "I've been waitin' to do this since I first laid eyes on you, buster," and started for Palmer.

Sam moved toward Palmer, put his left hand on Palmer's shoulder, and spun him around. At the same time, he drove a fist into Palmer's exposed jaw. It was so swift and savage that Palmer didn't even see it coming. His legs folded and he was unconscious as he fell on his back.

"I wanted to do that all day," Les said. "Why *you?*"

"You'd have cut him up," Sam said calmly. "Cable would wonder why."

After supper that Friday night, Sistie quickly did the dishes, went onto the back porch, got the watering can, returned to the house pump, filled it, and began watering the garden now that the heat of the day had diminished.

Her neighbor, Lily Christopher, was watering her garden, which abutted the common fence, as did Sistie's. They greeted each other as old friends and then Lily came over to the fence. She was a woman in her early thirties, married to Dave Christopher, who was a watermason by trade and some years older than she. A full-bodied, overweight woman with brown straight hair tied in a bun at the nape of her neck, she was resigned to the fact that her long, thin-lipped face reminded her of a horse's face.

Leaning on the fence post closest to Sistie, she said, "You're like me. Get it done tonight because tomorrow will be a long day, it looks like."

"The town will be jammed," Sistie agreed.

"Get your Pa to bed early, Sistie. He'll have a busy day with all the drunks. Somebody takin' you, or would you like to go with us?"

"Well, Sam Dana and I thought we'd take it in together."

Lily shook her head and smiled. "My, that man does get around with the girls, doesn't he?"

Sistie was suddenly alert. "I don't know and haven't heard. Does he?"

"Well, coming home this evening Dave passed him and Rita Dana in a buggy east of town."

"He's her brother-in-law. That's not so strange."

"That's *some* strange," Lily said tartly. "Her husband kicked her off Bar D because he couldn't trust her with the crew when he was gone, they say. Maybe she's shopping around."

"Sam only got home a week ago, and maybe he hasn't had a chance to see her."

"He knows where she lives. He knows where she works. All he had to do was stop by the store and say hello. Maybe he just wants her alone."

"That's possible," Sistie said reluctantly.

"Well, you know those Mexican women. They're Catholic. And they're trashy. They can confess their sins to a priest and then start acting bad all over again."

The conversation was becoming so uncomfortable to Sistie that she picked up the watering can, saying, "I'd better get started on this, Lily."

"Me too," Lily said, turned, and waddled back to her garden.

As Sistie started watering she went over her conversation with Lily. This news of a buggy ride with Rita was not only disturbing but it angered her. If Sam had time to drive out in the country with Rita, then he had time for an evening drive with her. Penned up in that hot courthouse office all day was dull and tiring and a buggy ride any evening would be a treat.

And what had Lily meant by saying Walt couldn't trust her with the crew when he was gone? Did he suspect her of infidelities with the crew? Sistie felt a faint nausea when she tried to picture this, and now Sam had brazenly driven Rita through town and out to Sam's private rendezvous. Was Sam just another lover for her to enjoy while she was protected by the bonds of marriage?

Abruptly Sistie remembered the whispered gossip among the girls in high school. It was the year Rita graduated and the story was that Rita, along with a couple of her girl and boy classmates, had driven out to Hacker's Pond in rented buggies after dark. At the pond, the story went, the girls had undressed at the eastern end of the pond while the boys stripped at the western end. Then the boys and girls waded out and joined. Nobody could prove the story that the girls had come back with wet hair. When questioned, the boys only smiled and said they'd gone for a buggy ride.

Her watering can was empty. She went back and refilled it and she found that her hands were trembling. It was not from fatigue but from an unreasoning anger. If he favored loose women of Rita's ilk, why should she be seen in his company? After all, she had a reputation in this town as a good girl, a reputation she treasured. If she was seen with him at the anniversary celebration, wouldn't the town think he was on another conquest with every hope of success? When she saw him tomorrow she would plead illness. But no, that was a liar's way out. She would face him down with the truth and simply refuse to be seen with him, for reasons she would mention.

12

At daybreak a tremendous shot of giant powder wakened the town and could be heard as far away as Bar D. At breakfast, at Sam's insistence, Les announced to the crew that this would be a day free of all work. Whoever wanted to go to town and hear the speech-making and watch the celebration could do so. Also at Sam's direction, Les told the Circle P pair that they could saddle up and their guns would be given to them and they could ride out.

As Carmichael and Steve hesitated, uncertain what to do next, Sam said, "Comin' into town with me, Les?"

Les looked at Carmichael and Steve, saying, "No, Sam. I'll stay here and keep the store." He still looked at the pair and added, "There just might be another fire. You can never tell."

Afterward, Sam changed into clean Levis and shirt, saddled up his horse, and rode into town with a couple of his crew, leaving them and taking the street to Cable's house.

Sistie answered his knock, opened the door, and unsmilingly said, "Mornin', Sam. Come in," and headed back for the kitchen. Sam followed. He noticed that Sistie was wearing a simple housedress and supposed that she would change into something more special before they headed for the festivities.

In the kitchen, Sistie waved to the table with its two chairs and Sam glanced at the kitchen counter.

"You've taken the bread already?" he asked.

"Pa took it in on his way to work. Like some coffee?"

"No thanks," Sam said. Sistie headed for her chair and when she was seated Sam sat down.

"You're lookin' pretty sober this morning. Got troubles?"

"More than enough," Sistie said. She looked directly at him, saying, "Sam, I'm not going with you to the celebration."

"I thought you were looking forward to it," Sam said.

"I am, but not with you, Sam."

"What changed your mind? What have I done?"

"You know what you did," Sistie said. "I'm good enough to walk to church with you. But not good enough for a buggy ride in the country, like Rita is."

"So that's out," Sam said. "What about it?"

"Are you sparking her, Sam? She's still your brother's wife, isn't she?"

"We had some business to talk over. The store is no good for that and neither is her boarding house, so we went for a drive where we could talk alone."

"Talk about what?" Sistie asked coldly.

Sam felt a touch of irritation that he was careful to hide. "Have you seen Rita lately?"

"Of course not. Why on earth should I?"

"Well, she's down on her luck. I thought maybe I could help her some way."

"Are you saying you gave her money? I can believe she'd ask for it."

"Whoa now," Sam said chidingly. Then he told her matter-of-factly about Rita's impoverished situation and about his suggestion that she take Walt to court for non-support. A reasonable solution to her present predicament. He finished by saying, "She's broke and Walt should be required to support her."

Sistie said dryly, "No, you didn't give her money. You just told her how to get it out of Walt."

Sam asked quietly, "What's biting you, Sistie?"

"Rita's no good and never has been, if you'll remember! I don't blame Walt for kicking her out! If I were a man I would too!"

"Tell me why."

Anger made Sistie's tone of voice rise a little as she said vehemently, "She's a cheap Mexican flirt! Aren't you really trying to help her just so you can hurt Walt?"

Sam looked at her carefully and read a cold, calculated anger in her always-pretty face. He thought, *This gal is a little bit crazy; none of what she's saying does she know to be true, only gossip, and intended to shame me!*

He put both his hands on the table and pushed himself to his feet. "You've missed it, Sistie. Even after I've told you Rita deserves better than she's got."

"She deserves exactly what she's got. She deserves even more of the same," Sistie said flatly, and she rose too, still facing him. "I'm trying to figure out why you care about Rita. You say you do, but why?"

From down the street came the second loud blast of giant powder, followed immediately by a band starting out on the first bars of the "Star Spangled Banner." The anniversary celebration was under way.

"Walk you to the concert?" Sam asked without much enthusiasm.

"No, thank you. I've already told Dave and Lily I'd go with them," Sistie said.

"I'll see you sometime," Sam said, picked up his hat, and headed out the kitchen, through the hall, and quietly let himself out the front door.

Sam mounted his horse, swearing softly, and headed for Main Street. He was relieved that he could duck the dinner and the inevitable speeches following it, but he was still both angered and puzzled at this sudden about-face of Sistie's. Perhaps she had arrived at her decision not to allow him to take her to the anniversary celebration out of some feminine logic that still baffled him. Having seen her three times in the past week, he had begun to think she was both attractive and pleasant to be with, but the eruption this morning surprised him. What he had thought had been an act of helpfulness to Rita, Sistie had interpreted as a lover's tryst with a tinge of sordidness.

Without even questioning why he did so, he headed for Cy Allen's office through the crowded streets. Stores and streets were emptying of buggies and wagons headed for the church but the tie rails in front of the saloons and Garrison House were jammed with horses. As he turned down the sidestreet he saw that the tie rail in front of Cy's office was empty. He was sure that Cy, as county judge, would be a participant and probably speech-maker this afternoon, but perhaps he could catch him on this Saturday morning in his office before the celebration really got under way.

When he tried the door he was pleased to find that it was unlocked. Nobody was in the waiting room, but Cy's office door was open. He went on through the waiting room, approached the office, and through its doorway saw Cy in shirtsleeves leafing through some papers at his desk. At the sound of his footsteps Cy looked up, smiled, and said, "Why aren't you in a nice cool saloon where everybody else is, Sam?"

Sam went in, took off his hat, and said, "That's where I'm headed after I talk with you. Can I interrupt?"

"Welcome and yes, definitely. Sit down, my friend, and tell me what's on your mind."

Sam took his accustomed chair, put his hat on the floor, and said, "It's Rita. What about her?"

"I talked with her and I'm representing her. I even talked with Howard Olsen earlier today. This is a tort, Sam, not a criminal offense, and I can represent her."

"Good, that's settled. Now tell me what I do about my other problem." He went on to tell Cy of Les and his crew's interception of Palmer and Carmichael and of Bar D's crew disarming them, taking them back to the ranch, and putting them to work cleaning up the ruins of the Big House.

Cy grinned and said, "Totally illegal, but understandable."

Then Sam told him of Steve's request to Les for permission to talk with the boss in private. He described Steve's sparring around before he asked what it was worth to Sam in money if he told the DA or whoever that Walt had not been with the old crew from noon until the move to Circle P. Sam had given a flat refusal to bribe him. Then Les, who had heard their conversation through an open window, came into the room and said he was a witness to the whole conversation. Sam told of slugging Steve Palmer to keep Les from beating up the man. Sam finished by saying that Palmer and Carmichael were in town now and asked, "What do I do about that, Cy?"

"Go to Raunce, the district attorney, and right now."

"What'll happen?"

"Palmer will be picked up, arrested, and put in protective custody until the trial." He added, "The damn fool. He's as good as dead." He reached into the top drawer of his desk, brought out a sheet of paper, and stretched out a hand for the pen in the inkwell on the desktop.

"I'll give you a note, Sam, to Cable or Raunce. Don't leave it with the hired help. Give it to one or the other."

While Cy wrote on the sheet of paper Sam wondered if there was even a faint chance that he would catch Cable or Raunce in the courthouse, and he doubted it. Cy looked at the wall clock, noted the time, and wrote it down. Then he folded the sheet of paper and shoved it toward Sam, saying, "It's the wrong day. But make a try."

Sam picked up the folded paper and put it in his shirt pocket, then asked, "Where's Walt? No idea?"

"Nope. A rented room somewhere. Cable might know, if you could find him. And you can't."

Steve and Carmichael rode into the thronged town together. At the first saloon Steve said to Carmichael, "Let's see Olsen and see where we can find Walt."

He pulled in on the crowded tie rail and before dismounting Steve said, "I won't take long. I'll see you at the hotel bar in a few minutes."

Both dismounted and separated. Carmichael headed for the hotel saloon and Steve went off to Olsen's office. Steve opened the street door and stepped into the waiting room where Olsen was talking to three seated punchers. Olsen, recognizing him as one of Walt's old crew, excused himself, rose, and came over to Steve. They did not shake hands but Olsen smiled pleasantly and asked, "In town for the hurrah?"

Steve nodded. "That's right, but first I'd like to talk to the boss, if I could find out where he is."

Olsen tilted his head back, looked at the ceiling briefly, and said, "Upstairs, to your right as you go out."

Steve thanked him but Olsen was already headed back for the three punchers.

Outside, Steve found the covered stairway and climbed it. He tried the door at the head of the landing, found it locked, and then he knocked sharply on the door.

"Who is it?" Walt's voice called from behind the door.

"Me, Steve Palmer, Walt. Gotta talk with you."

He heard the bolt slam back, the door opened, and Walt smiled faintly. "How in the hell did you find me?"

"Olsen told me."

"Well, come in. Never liked drinkin' alone anyway." Both men stepped into a small but comfortable living room. There was a bottle and glass on the rectangular table that faced the sofa.

"No time for that, boss. I just came to warn you."

"What about?"

"Somebody seen you the night of the fire and got the word to Sam. Sam's likely on his way right now to see Cable."

Walt swore with a bitter savagery. "Who was it?"

"I tell you I don't know. Likely some rider cuttin' across Bar D on his way home from town."

"How'd you find out?" Walt demanded.

"I stopped by to pick up some gear I left. The new cook told me." He shook his head. "You'd better get out while you still can, Walt, and to hell with not leaving the county."

"Yeah," Walt said solemnly. "Can you get me my horse from the feed stable?"

"I got no money, boss."

Walt reached into his hip pocket, drew out a snap purse, took out an eagle, and handed it to Steve. Immediately Steve started for the door, saying, "I'll tie him down at the foot of the stairs. Now you take care, boss."

Steve went down the stairs two steps at a time, turned left, and went upstreet into the saloon. He found Carmichael, gave him the eagle, and told him to bring Walt's horse back to the stairs, then get Walt at Olsen's apartment. He himself was going on an errand for Walt.

Alone now at Bar D, Les headed past the diminished rubble heap for the barn. In its half-dark coolness he

climbed up to the seat of the buckboard that was closest
to the open doorway. Now he reviewed what had happened last night with Steve and the probabilities of what
would happen today. He was reasonably certain of
Steve's present thinking. Steve needed him dead because
he had heard Steve's bribe offer to Sam. Steve knew that
he was alone now and there would never be a better
chance to silence him. Les also remembered that Steve
knew Bar D and its approaches far better than he did.
Steve's approach very probably would be from the foothills and rough country to the north. Would he wait for
night? Les wondered. Unlikely, for most of the crew,
drunk or sober, would show up by suppertime. Then
Steve's try would have to be soon and in daylight.

Would he enlist Carmichael as his accomplice? Les
doubted it. He wouldn't be that big a fool. Only one man
could testify against him, and without him the rest would
simply be hearsay.

Les stirred himself now, heading for the little house,
where he found his carbine, checked the loads, and
tramped back to the barn. He climbed up the ladder to
the hayloft where both double doors were opened to the
east and west. Here he took up his vigil facing the north-
west, where he could see not only the bunkhouse and
little house but the long reaches of rolling country that
ended in the foothills.

He lost track of time and paid attention to the sights
and sounds. The horses in the corral moved occasionally
but their hoofbeats were not sustained.

It was midafternoon and he was drawing on the last of
his patience when he heard the sound of a dislodged rock,
the direction of which was not identifiable.

Within his view nothing had moved except an occasional bird on the wing.

While he was trying to puzzle this out he heard the

sound of the horses in the corral moving and then came a subdued whinny from one of the corraled horses. Were the horses just playing around or was this some sort of signal that he should be able to read? He listened carefully and could hear only his own breathing. Impatient, he rose now and took a step toward the door that looked down on the corral. A floorboard creaked under his weight and he halted. The sun beating down on an unshaded wooden building would make expanded wood give the same noise, but the sound of footsteps was different. He stood where he was, listening.

Then he heard the unmistakable creak of wood bearing weight and he knew instantly that someone was mounting the ladder to the loft. In less time than it took to form the words in his mind he thought then, *Palmer, he was watching and saw me come in here.* He moved back into the hay, discarded his rifle in it, took off his hat, covered it, drew his gun, cocked it, and then lay belly down and quietly pulled the hay over himself. The creaking ladder ground out the soft swish of the hay when he moved it.

Then he heard the first footfall on the heavy board floor. The footsteps came closer, passed him, and halted in the barn's open doorway.

Ever so slowly he moved the hay off his face and was looking at Steve Palmer's back. Palmer's rifle dangled from his right hand as he surveyed most of Bar D.

Les knew instantly that Palmer had not seen him enter the barn, or he would have been far more cautious in his approach to the door.

Les pointed his six-gun at Steve and then said, "You're covered, Palmer. Throw that rifle out the door."

He was coming to his feet as Palmer whirled and lifted his rifle, cocking it as he swung around and began to lift it.

Les shot without aiming. His slug caught Palmer in the

body and drove him two steps backward and out the door. Palmer yelled as he fell and then the sound of his body smashing into the ground was plain to hear.

Les ran for the ladder, not even looking out the door. He descended swiftly, three rungs at a time, landing upright in the dust, ran out the door, and turned right and headed for the corner of the barn. Rounding it, he saw Palmer flat on his back in the dust, his rifle some feet beyond his head. Cautiously now, Les moved toward him, his gun at the ready.

When he had reached Palmer, who was hatless now, Les saw the odd, awry angle of his head on his neck. Coming closer, Les looked at the still figure on the ground. Blood was staining the midsection of Palmer's shirt but he made no move. Eyes wide open to the sky were unseeing and he knew immediately that his bullet had not killed Palmer. His neck had been broken instantly on impact with the ground.

He knelt now, reached out, and put his fingers on Palmer's jugular vein. He picked up a slowing, fading heartbeat and waited until it stopped, then rose, swearing softly. At what, he didn't know; or perhaps it was out of relief that it was Palmer instead of himself. Palmer had been out to kill him and been killed instead, it was that simple.

Returning to the barn, he found a canvas of a bed in one of the wagons and went back with it to Steve's body. After spreading the canvas over the dead man, he went back to the buckboard, pulled it outside, and then headed for the corral and a horse. He would give Cable in town his look at Steve Palmer.

The drive into Garrison was a strange one for Les. Before he reached the outskirts of Garrison he met people he knew but did not stop to exchange pleasantries. If anyone guessed what the canvas-wrapped bundle covered they did not ask. Besides, on a day of celebration like this a death was unthinkable.

Les headed for the alley that ran behind Plover's Hardware Store, pulled up at the loading platform, and went through the big open door that led into the storeroom. He came out some minutes later followed by two clerks, one of whom was carrying a cloth stretcher.

Les watched them unload the body into the stretcher and climb the stairs with it, and then they halted by him.

"Told Cable about this?" the older man asked.

"I'm on my way now to find him," Les said, and climbed back into the buckboard.

At the courthouse he found the sheriff's office locked but, on his way out, standing on the courthouse steps, he could hear the band music and applause from the crowd on the church lawn.

Searching through that crowd for Sheriff Cable he knew would be a long and fruitless job, probably. Then he remembered that Steve Palmer and Carmichael had been summoned by lawyer Olsen.

He found a place for the buckboard close to Olsen's office and then headed for it. He was sure Olsen would be at the speech-making but it was worth a try. At Olsen's office he found the door unlocked and stepped into the waiting room. There he found Olsen and Sheriff Cable in conversation. Both were seated but at his entrance they rose. Les saw no reason for asking for privacy for his conversation with Sheriff Cable. He thumbed back his hat off his forehead, nodded to both men, and moved toward them, saying, "You heard yet, Mort?"

"No. What is it?"

"About a half hour ago I brought a dead man into Plover's. Name's Steve Palmer. Reckon you could say I killed him."

"I talked to him about an hour and a half ago," Olsen said. "What happened?"

Les began at the beginning, describing his crew's capture of Palmer and Carmichael and taking them back to Bar D and working them, against their protests. This morning, he said, Sam had given him orders to let them go. He himself elected to stay at Bar D instead of coming in for the celebration. Palmer had heard him make that decision before both Circle P men headed for town. He interrupted his account by asking Cable abruptly, "Talked with Sam today, Mort?"

Cable shifted his arm in its canvas sling and said, "Yes, he found me. Why?"

"He tell you about me overhearing Palmer say that Walt wasn't with his crew like they claim he was?"

"That's what Cy Allen's letter said. Sam said, too, that Palmer asked for a bribe to keep his mouth shut. You heard him, Sam said."

Les nodded. "So that makes me the only witness to what Steve told Sam."

"All right. What about it?" Cable said.

"That's why Steve came gunnin' for me out at Bar D this afternoon. He wanted me dead."

"What happened out there?" Cable asked.

Les told him then of his wait in the hayloft for Palmer. He had chosen the loft because all the ranch buildings were in sight. Apparently, Palmer, on his manhunt, had chosen the loft for the same reason. Les described how he had hidden in the hay and had heard Steve Palmer climb the ladder and head for the open haymow doors just as Les had done and for the same reason. He finished by saying, "I got the drop on him but he wanted to shoot it out. I shot first. He fell back through the loft doorway. The fall broke his neck. So I reckon you could say I killed him."

"Before he killed you, you mean," Cable said.

Les only nodded.

Cable picked up his hat and said, "Let's have a look over at Plover's." He put on his hat and said, "I don't reckon you've heard about Walt?" As Les shook his head in negation, Cable said, "He lit out. He's gone."

"You think Palmer told him about me bein' a witness?"

"Palmer manhuntin' you and Walt lightin' a shuck kinda fit together, don't they?"

"Too damn well," Les said.

Cable said to Olsen, "Better come along, Howard. After all, you sent for Palmer."

Just before six o'clock, when the town was emptying of its Saturday-evening crowd, Sam went into Safford's Dry Goods and walked to the dress goods counter, where Rita was just finishing waiting on a woman. When the customer had gone Sam moved up to Rita and said, "Quittin' time, isn't it?"

"Yes, thank the Lord," she said.

"You didn't know it before, but you do now. You're having supper with me at the hotel."

Rita smiled tiredly and asked, "Does that include a small drink before we eat?"

Sam grinned and said, "Before we eat and after we eat, if you want it." He looked at her. She was wearing a green-checked gingham dress and the same red cardigan she had last worn.

"I'll meet you out front, Sam. I have to check out my cash drawer."

Sam waited outside and presently Rita joined him and they headed through the crowd for the hotel.

Sam walked across the lobby, spoke to the desk clerk, and was given a key to the room always saved for him if possible. He and Rita went down the hall to his room, and Sam opened the door and showed her in. He was careful to leave the door open, which was expected of a male guest entertaining a woman. Sam opened the window as Rita took off her cardigan in the warm room and seated herself in the easy chair closest to two others that flanked the bed.

It seemed only seconds before a waiter carried a tray loaded with two glasses, a pitcher of ice and water, and a bottle of labeled whiskey.

Sam mixed two dark brown drinks diluted with a little water and set Rita's on the bedside table. As they had their drinks they talked about the noisy day and the sporadic applause for who knew which speaker. Finished with their drinks, they left the room and headed down the corridor for the dining room, which seemed to be about half full. After looking at the chalked blackboard by the door, which announced the supper menu, they were shown by a head waiter to a wall table for two and they placed their dinner orders. While they were waiting, Rita told him of her hectic day in the store. In exchange, Sam told her of his, omitting any mention of his meeting with Sistie Cable that morning. Instead, he told her then of Les's prank of yesterday in intercepting two of Walt's crew on their way to town and forcing them to work on the burned house.

Their suppers came and they were just beginning to eat when Howard Olsen stopped at their table. He put a hand on Sam's shoulder to keep him from rising and said, "Evening, Sam and Rita. Quite a day, wasn't it?" When they both agreed it had been, Olsen said, "I've got some news for both of you. When you're finished supper, why don't you both stop by my office."

When Sam agreed, Olsen waved a lazy goodbye and left the dining room.

"What could that be about?" Rita asked.

"Well, Cy talked with him this morning. Maybe we'll find out about what."

Finished with their supper, they left the hotel and headed downstreet in the dusk.

A lamp was lit in Olsen's waiting room and Olsen came out of his office to usher them to two easy chairs facing his desk.

When they were seated, Olsen sat down behind his table desk. "Sam, I'm sure you've talked with Cy about our meeting this morning."

Sam nodded. "He said he was representing Rita and that's about all."

"He didn't tell you that Walt skipped town, because that happened after we talked."

"Does that surprise you?" Sam asked.

"Everything I've seen and heard today surprises me. For instance, your new foreman, Les Beecham, brought in a dead man today."

"One of my crew?" Sam asked swiftly.

"No, Steve Palmer." He told of the confrontation between Les and Palmer in the hayloft of the barn.

"Does Cable know?"

"He knows and he's not holding Les. After all, Palmer came out to your place to gun down Les and kill him." Olsen shifted in his chair and said, "Let's talk about you, Rita. Walt's jumping town changes what Cy and I agreed on this morning. Walt is to provide you with a house and a-hundred-dollars-a-month support. I don't think either of us will see Walt for a while, but it doesn't matter all that much."

"Who pays for the house and who pays the hundred dollars a month if Walt's gone?" Sam asked.

"First I checked with Pete O'Hara, he's the city magistrate. I told him of my agreement with Cy as to what

Rita was to get. He wrote out a court order and we went to the bank together and saw Jess Wilford." Now he looked at Rita. "Drop by the bank on Monday and open an account with Wilford. Either of you have any questions?"

"No questions," Rita said, and looked first at Olsen and then Sam. "Just my thanks to you both for helping me out."

Sam rose, saying, "Send me your bill, Howard."

"There will be no bill, Sam. It was my pleasure. And I should have tended to it long before this."

They said goodnight and then Sam stepped out onto the dark, uncrowded boardwalk. Rita was silent for so long that Sam finally said, "Something troubling you?"

"No, I'm just stunned, Sam. Stop a second." When Sam did she put her hands on his shoulders and kissed him on the mouth. "That's for making life worth living again."

Sam walked her back to the boarding house and now she was full of chatter. She was speculating on the small houses she knew about and said she would spend tomorrow looking them over and that she'd tell him what she'd found. At the door of the boarding house, they shook hands and said goodnight.

As he walked to Safford's, where he had left his horse at the tie rail, he felt a pleasantly warm affection for Rita. It was always a good feeling to see someone's hard luck change to good luck, especially if that person was as deserving as Rita. During the last hour she had changed from a grim and worried woman into a happy and radiant one. He only hoped that Olsen had his facts right concerning Wilford's promise to take care of Rita on Pete O'Hara's assurance.

As he was untying his horse he wondered if he should prowl the town, looking for Les Beecham. His decision was immediate. There was no need to, for Les, with his deep sense of responsibility, would have headed back to Bar D to count off the crew to see if any were missing.

At Bar D Sam saw that the lamps were on in the house. He was heading for the corral when Les called from the darkness by the house, "Leave 'im here, Sam. I'll take care of it."

When Sam put in at the tie rail and went into the lamp-lit house, Les was gone. Sam scarcely had time to throw his hat on the living-room sofa and shuck out of his boots before Les came in the opposite door.

Sam, in the dim lamplight, could see no immediate concern in Les's appearance or actions. Les swung a chair out from the table, put it close to the sofa, and said, "Big day out here, Sam. Hear about it?"

"I heard. This was your lucky day, my friend. Tell me all of it."

Les sat down and told for the second time today of his and Steve Palmer's mutual manhunt.

When Sam heard him out he said, "No thought of a charge on Cable's part, or you wouldn't be here."

"It was like he said, 'Just go home and forget it. I know where to find you.'"

Sam only nodded and was silent a long moment before he said, "Guess where Walt is?"

"Not at Circle P," Les said. "He's on the high lonesome, I'd reckon."

"Not for long," Sam said. "Know Hugh Ransome?"

"U.S. marshal in Ridgeway, you mean? No, I don't."

"Neither do I, but we will," Sam said. He rose now, rammed both hands into his hip pockets, and began to slowly pace the open space between the sofa and the front door. As he turned and came back toward Les he halted and asked, "Why don't we do Cable's job for him?"

"You mean gettin' Walt on the run?" Les asked. At Sam's nod he continued, "If you're thinking of Ransome, it won't work, Sam. In these parts a U.S. marshal doesn't act unless a county sheriff asks him to."

"He can act on an Indian reservation, because that's federal property."

Les nodded. "Tell me what you're gettin' at."

"Just what you were getting at. But didn't go far enough. Walt forged those bills of sale and Rita can prove it."

"Somewhere I've heard a wife ain't allowed to testify against her husband."

"In court, you mean," Sam said.

"I don't know what I mean, Sam. You're a hell of a lot closer to bein' a lawyer than I am."

"But she won't testify in court. She must have saved some letters and I think she'll show me and even give me them to show Ransome."

"Isn't that testifyin' against him?"

"Not in court," Sam said. "This will never get to court. All this will be is showing a U.S. marshal that those forged bills of sale were written and signed by Walt Dana. That's grounds for two arrests—Walt for forging signatures and the agent's for accepting the bills of sale."

"So where does that get us?"

"It gets us out of Campbell County and into the rest of the United States. Tomorrow morning I see Rita and then we take off for Ridgeway."

13

Sam was up before daylight and didn't wake Les. The lamp in the cook-shack kitchen was lighted and Sam was fed a cold steak sandwich and coffee by the cook before he lit a lantern and headed for the corral to catch and saddle up his horse.

It was full daylight by the time he reached Rita's boarding house and he noted that lamps were lit in the kitchen and dining room although Sunday morning was when everybody slept late. This was especially true after yesterday's celebration, but he had a hunch that Rita would be up early so as to get on with her house-hunting. Tying his horse to the ring at the stepping block, he did not ring the doorbell but tried the door and found it unlocked. Apparently Mr. Petty had heard the door open, for he came from the kitchen and through the dining room. When Mr. Petty saw him he said, "Mornin', Sam. You're up pretty early. Want some breakfast?"

"Already had it, Ralph. I'd like to wait in your parlor until Rita comes down."

"Want the Mrs. to wake her?"

"Don't bother. She'll be down early, I think."

"Like some coffee while you wait?" Sam said no thanks and Petty gestured toward the parlor. "Take a chair. If she comes down the back stairs I'll tell her you're here."

Sam took a chair in the parlor where he could watch the stairs and put his hat on his knees. He heard talk in the kitchen and then Rita came into sight from the kitchen. She was carrying a cup of coffee but the surprise of hearing of his presence was still on her face.

"Morning, Sam. What brings you in so early?"

Sam was on his feet now and he said, "Got a long day ahead of me, Rita. Good morning to you."

"Has something happened?" Rita asked swiftly.

Sam shook his head, gesturing toward the couch. "Why don't we sit there? You can put your coffee down on the end table."

Rita crossed the room, set her coffee on the table, and sat down. Sam moved over and slacked onto the couch beside her. "I figured you'd be house-hunting so I came in early."

"I will be. What is it, Sam?"

"This is a crazy question, especially at this hour. First, though, drink some of your coffee."

"I'll let it cool off a minute." And then she asked again, "What is it?"

"All right, does Walt ever write you, Rita?"

"Not since I've been in town. He used to, though."

"If you kept the letters I suppose they were burned in the fire."

"No, I brought some old letters here with me. I guess I wanted to make sure I'm still married to him. Why do you ask?"

"I need a sample of his handwriting. If everything hadn't been burned in the house I wouldn't be bothering you."

"Are you going to make trouble for him, Sam?"

"All I can, and why not? You don't need to know any more than that. He's made nothing but trouble for you, for me, for Cy Allen, and for Howard Olsen. I think he's earned some trouble for himself."

"Can you tell me what kind of trouble?"

"No, I can't. I don't want you to know anything about it."

"It's his rustling, isn't it?"

"No comment," Sam said.

Rita rose then, saying, "I'll be down in a minute," and crossed the room and climbed the stairway.

Sam rose and began to slowly pace the parlor. Another early breakfaster came down from the second floor, saw him, said good morning, and went into the dining room.

Rita came down the stairs then and Sam went over to her. She extended a sheaf of letters all in their envelopes and bound together with a length of yarn. She extended them to Sam, who accepted them, nodded, and said, "You'll get them back."

Rita said nothing, only shrugged her slim shoulders.

Sam went back for his hat, picked it up, and said, "Well, happy house-hunting. Keep in touch now, and thanks."

Outside, he stuffed the pack of letters into his saddlebag before mounting and heading back for Bar D.

At the ranch, Les was waiting, his horse saddled and tied under the big pine. As Sam dismounted Les came over from the house. "Any luck with the letters?"

"All we need," Sam answered.

After putting their horses up at the feed stable in Ridgeway, Sam and Les headed back downstreet for the Brewer County Courthouse. Sam, saddlebag with the letters slung over his shoulder, halted on the boardwalk in front of the courthouse and said to Les, "You know Ransome?"

"By sight. But never met him."

"I better do the talking, then," Sam said, and moved through the courthouse doors. U.S. Marshal Hugh Ransome's office in the Brewer County Courthouse was immediately to the right of the entrance. The sign above the first door proclaimed U.S. MARSHAL, and below it *Hugh Ransome* in smaller and more modest letters. That was a good omen, Sam thought, for he had put the authority of his office above his own identity.

Although the corner office was the largest in the courthouse it was sparsely furnished, with two flat-top desks facing each other, one on either side of a big double window. At the far desk and facing the doorway sat a long-bodied man under middle-age who looked up from the paperwork on his desk as they entered and then stood up. He was taller than either Sam or Les, with hooded bright green eyes above an aquiline nose and a roan-colored full mustache that made his cheeks seem gaunt to emaciation. His hair was short cut and so red it was almost orange.

Stepping out from behind the desk, he put his hands on lean hips and said, "Afternoon, gentlemen. How can I help you? I'm Hugh Ransome."

Sam went forward first, introduced himself and shook hands, then introduced Les. There was already one chair facing the side of his desk and now Marshal Ransome swung out another chair from the conference table in the corner. All three men seated themselves as both Sam and Les briefly studied the marshal with open curiosity. Sam decided to plunge in with no preliminary small talk, so he asked, "How do I report a rustling operation that the law won't pay any attention to?"

Ransome gave him a look of mild surprise and asked, "What law?"

"Sheriff Cable in Campbell County. Sheriff Munson isn't involved. You are, because it's in your judicial district."

Ransome picked up a pencil from his desk, drew a clean sheet of paper from the right-hand drawer, and said, "Back up a little, Mr. Dana. Who's doing the rustling and who's lost beef, and—"

"I have," Les said.

"Are you accusing some specific person?"

Les tilted his head toward Sam and said, "Yes, his half brother, Walt Dana."

Ransome looked from Les to Sam and then carefully put down his pencil. "I don't see how that involves my office. In other words, why do you come to me?"

Sam answered, "Because the Indian agent on the reservation bought stolen beef and is reselling it to small ranchers across the mountains. Does that involve you?"

"Of course, if it's true. Now tell me what evidence you have."

Sam looked at Les and said, "You tell him, Les."

Les told him then of trailing some of his stolen beef over the mountains to the reservation. Walt Dana, he said, forged his name to a false bill of sale, which the agent accepted. He also forged other names to bills of sale for other stolen cattle.

Ransome heard him out and then said with a wry skepticism, "Can you prove any of this?"

"I've proven it to myself. You can prove it in a court of law," Les said.

"Just exactly how?" the marshal asked.

Sam reached over for his saddlebag, opened the flap, and took out the package of Walt's letters to Rita. He explained then that the handwriting in Walt's letters would verify that it was the same handwriting on the forged bills of sale that were in the Indian agent's files. He concluded by saying, "These letters won't mean a thing to you until you see the bills of sale Walt gave the agent."

Ransome slipped one of the letters from the pack, took

the letter from the envelope, and read it. Then he looked over at Sam and said, "Where'd you get these?"

"From Rita Dana. Walt's wife."

Ransome frowned. "A wife can't testify against her husband in court. The law forbids it."

"If you bring it into court she'll testify that that's his handwriting. Nothing more. She won't be testifying against him, only identifying the handwriting."

Ransome looked at him for a long moment and then said, "No different than identifying a weapon or a person is what you're saying, isn't it?"

"I guess I am. If you think the handwriting in the letters matches up with the bills of sale, then you'll do the charging, she won't."

Ransome sighed. "I think you're right. It has no bearing on Walt Dana's guilt or innocence in rustling cattle. Like to ride over to the reservation with me tomorrow, both of you?"

"That's why we're here," Sam said quietly. "I'll leave the letters with you. Look them over tonight and try and get the hang of his writing. We'll take them with us, of course."

While Ransome was eating his early morning breakfast, the kitchen was making up sandwiches for the ride over to Fort Walker on the reservation. Sandwiches packed in his saddlebag, Ransome headed for the hotel and saw two horses at the tie rail with Dana and Beecham waiting under the boardwalk's wooden awning. They exchanged greetings and Ransome said, "I know where the reservation is but I reckon Beecham knows a short-cut to it."

"That I do," Les said. The three men mounted, headed downstreet, and turned west for the mountains and reservations beyond, Ransome riding in the middle.

The flats still held the night's cool and the horses were frisky and eager. When they finally settled into a steady pace Ransome said, "Well, I did my homework on those letters last night." He looked at Sam. "Your brother's not only ornery but he's an ornery writer too."

"School was always for other kids, not for Walt," Sam said. They settled into a steady pace and Les set a course a little south of west.

Presently Ransome said, "Never met your half brother. Tell me about him."

Sam did and Les tactfully kept silent. When they were in the foothill timber Les took the lead and after an hour's ride they came onto the wagon-and-stage road that crossed the mountains. Except for a midmorning stage headed east, they saw only an occasional deer or two that bounded across the road and into the tall timber. Over the crest of the mountains they picked up a small stream which in turn picked up other creeks. They nooned on the banks of a sizable stream and, after watering their horses, they ate their sandwiches and then headed downslope again.

Now Ransome was full of questions, which he put to Les, who answered that the agent's name was Mitchell Baines and had been the agent for the last ten to twelve years, a heavyset man with a ponderous belly and a black beard. It seemed to Ransome that Les was being extremely careful to be fair to Baines, but the marshal could remember Les's accusation yesterday against Baines. Today Les did not elaborate but Ransome got the message.

After splashing through several feeder streams they came to the main stream, which Les called Falling River, and they were in the spruce that shadowed the old wreckage of beaver lodges long since hunted out and mostly washed out.

Lower down, when they hit the piñon and cedar above

the flats, they had their first distant look at the reservation. They saw tepees scattered across the green flats on either side of some log buildings. As they rode closer they saw that, ahead, the river which turned south was joined by a smaller river coming from the north that was bridged. Beyond it there was a big square building of weathered logs. When they crossed the bridge in a racket of horses' hooves on wooden planking it was plain that the big building was a trading post whose second floor was a hotel. Downriver a hundred yards from it was a two-story log house with a one-story addition attached to it. Big cottonwoods flanked the agency building and the riverbanks. In the now hot and windless afternoon they could see the flag hanging limply from the flagpole in front of the agency. There was a tie rail in the shade of the cottonwoods and Les, leading again, headed for it. As Sam and Ransome dismounted at the tie rail, Les remained in the saddle. When Ransome looked at him quizzically he said, "You won't want me right away, Marshal. I've been snooping in there and Baines would remember me. Just ask for the files on bills of sale."

"That's all I ask for?"

"The bills of sale themselves, not the register book. He tried that on me and he'll try it on you."

"I read you right."

"Me, I'm headin' for the cracker barrel in the store. See you some later."

Sam and Ransome watched him head across the hard-packed dirt for the trading post and Ransome observed, "You've got a spunky foreman there, Sam."

"That's what I think, too."

Ransome lifted the saddlebag containing Rita's letters from behind his saddle and slung it over his shoulder. Together now, Sam and Ransome headed up the graveled walk and past the flagpole toward the door to the agency office.

The door was open and it let into a big room holding two rolltop desks back to back against the far wall. Ransome knocked firmly on the door frame and was bid enter with a gruff "Come in, come in."

As his eyes adjusted from sunlight to shade, it took only a couple of seconds for Ransome to identify the grossly fat figure seated at the desk facing the agency house. He had a gray-shot, full black beard that matched in coloration his thick hair. Incongruously, he wore a townsman's dark business suit.

As Ransome moved deliberately toward the agent he said, "I'm Hugh Ransome. U.S. Marshal for the seventh judicial district."

Before he had finished Baines had heaved his ponderous bulk to his feet, for he had already noticed the gold marshal's badge on Ransome's shirt pocket. "Heard a lot about you, Marshal, but you never seem to get out our way."

He extended his hand and the two men shook hands. Ransome introduced Sam, which brought a momentary flicker of interest to Baines's eyes, and they too shook hands. Baines gestured toward a cracked leather sofa against the wall just behind his desk. "Take a seat, gentlemen, and tell me what I can do for you."

He waited until Sam and Ransome had taken off their hats and seated themselves and then he slacked into his oversized chair, facing them.

"Well, it's like this," Ransome said almost carelessly. "I've had complaints that beef in Brewer and Campbell counties have been stolen, driven over the mountains, and sold to you for feeding your Indians. I'm sure there's no truth in that rumor or you'd have reported it."

"You can bet I would," Baines said flatly. "Every head

of cattle I buy here has to have a bill of sale to go with it." He half turned, pulled open the lowest drawer of the desk, and took out a good-sized ledger. With both hands he extended it to Ransome and said, "That's our register of purchasers' and owners' names. We don't keep track of the names of the Indians that receive beef branded such-and-such."

Sam spoke for the first time. "Why's that?"

The agent shook his head and smiled sadly. "Ever been on a reservation on beef-issue day?" When Sam shook his head in negation, Baines went on, "The Indians like to chase and hunt down their beef just like they did the buffalo. It keeps 'em happy because they're still hunters and they have the sport of the chase. Sometimes they'll chase a cow for miles before they'll bring it down. But they always get what's due them. We haven't got the manpower to check on which hunter gets a critter branded so-and-so, but nobody goes hungry. We see to that."

Sam only nodded but he noticed that Ransome was leafing through the register.

Now Ransome spoke. "This register seems to be in order. Weight of beef noted, brand noted, and name of seller noted along with price paid." He looked up from the register and said, "You keep all bills of sale for the stock you buy?"

"Certainly," Baines said. "It's required of me."

"Are they in this office?" Ransome asked.

Baines pointed over Sam's shoulder and said, "In those two file cabinets."

"I'd like a look at them," Ransome said.

"But they're in the register, Marshal. Why go to all that trouble?"

"A man could forge a bill of sale on beef that isn't his. Couldn't he?"

Baines hesitated. "Why, I suppose he could. I've never heard of it being done."

"I'd like a look at those bills of sale. Do I have to go to court to get a look at them?"

"You do not. Come look," Baines said.

He rose slowly and walked past Sam and Ransome to twin wooden file cabinets in the rear corner. In front of the file cabinets and against the outer wall was an oblong stout table beneath a square window, two chairs pushed up to it.

From the furthermost file cabinet he pulled open a drawer. He cleaned out the top drawer of twelve fat and heavy envelopes and stacked them on the table, saying, "One for each month of the year. If you want to go back further try the next drawer and the next and the next."

Ransome tossed his saddlebag on the table and said, "Much obliged. We won't be bothering you if we work here?"

"Certainly not," Baines said courteously. "I'll leave you alone while I do some business at the post."

When he had left the room both Sam and Ransome seated themselves and Ransome asked, "How far back did this rustling start, Sam?"

"I reckon it started this year. Why don't you take the top three and give me the next three."

Ransome nodded and divided the top six envelopes between them, while Sam took out Rita's letters from the saddlebag, giving Ransome three sample letters. He put three in front of him, took them from their envelopes, and spread them before him. Ransome did likewise.

Then the tedious part of the investigation began. Sam was resigned to spending hours at it. It was with a jolting surprise, however, when halfway through the bills of sale in the first envelope he came to a bill of sale made out to Walt Dana and signed by Tucker Davidson. The capital

*D*s in both names were separated from the following letter.

Sam compared the handwriting on the envelope of one of Walt's letters to Rita with Tucker Davidson's signature. Then he picked up the envelope and the bill of sale and said quietly, "Ransome, have a look," and extended the envelope and bill of sale to Ransome.

The marshal gave both pieces of paper careful scrutiny and then raised his glance to Sam. "Bull's-eye," Ransome said. "You've got it."

Within the next hour they had come up with four more forged bills of sale, signed in Walt's handwriting. Altogether, Walt had sold thirty-four head of cattle to Baines.

They were still searching for more forgeries when Baines returned from the trading post. Ransome let him settle his bulk in his chair before rising, gathering up the forged bills of sale, and moving over to Baines's desk. Sam rose too and trailed him.

Ransome put the papers and one of Rita's letters before Baines, saying mildly, "Have a look at these, will you?"

Baines looked at the bills of sale, then glanced up at Ransome. "They look all right to me. What's wrong with them?"

"The signatures on all those bills of sale were forged by Walt Dana. He stole the beef, forged the owners' signatures, and you paid him for the beef."

Baines leaned back in his chair, his glance still on Ransome. "Wait . . . a . . . minute," he said deliberately. "I never see the beef I buy. My foreman weighs the beef on correct agency scales, brings me bills of sale, and I make out a check to the seller. Sometimes I know him, sometimes I don't. Some ranchers want cash because the nearest banks are in Garrison and Ridgeway. That's a long ride to cash a check if you come from the west side of the reservation. Two days to get their money and two days back."

"If you give them cash then you must ask them for a signed receipt," Ransome said.

Baines nodded. "Which I promptly send to the Bureau in Washington."

"Don't you keep a record of who you pay cash to?"

"It's right in that register I first showed you."

"That could be doctored by you or your foreman."

Baines showed mild surprise, "Doctored, how?"

"I don't know now, but I will know. It'll take a little time but I'll find out."

Baines shrugged his thick shoulders and nodded. "I'm sure you will. You're the law and that's your job."

"On the evidence all three of us in this room have read, I'm going to issue a warrant for the arrest of Walt Dana for rustling."

14

ONE HUNDRED DOLLARS REWARD

For information leading to the apprehension and arrest of WALTER DANA, former co-owner of the Bar D ranch in Campbell County.

Dana is wanted by the undersigned United States Marshal for theft of cattle and illegal sale of same, of altering brands on stolen cattle, of falsifying bills of sale to Indian agents and their employees, and of suspected arson of ranch buildings not his own.

Physical Description: Dana is thirty-five years of age, six feet in height, 210 pounds in weight, blue eyes, sandy hair, ruddy complexion, beardless, scar on right cheek, carelessly dressed, and likely to be unshaven.

If possible, report where and when Walter Dana was last seen or where he can be located to the office of United States Marshal, Seventh Judicial District in Ridgeway, Brewer County.

Hugh Ransome, United States Marshal

When Walt looked up in the dim lamplight cast by the kitchen lamp he said in an anger-choked voice, "Where'd you get this?"

"I took it off the wall in the stage station in Ridgeway," Harry Carmichael said.

"How long was it up?" Walt asked.

"I don't know. Like I said, Munson stopped me when I was coming out of the hardware store. He says, 'Hear your boss is in trouble.' And I said, 'First I knew about it.' Then he said, 'Come on down to the office.' So I went with 'im. He had it tacked up on his bulletin board." He hesitated. "Want me to wake the boys?"

"No, what the hell for? What did he say about Ransome?"

"Him and Sam and Les went over to the reservation with a sample of your handwriting and talked with Baines."

"Is Baines under arrest?"

"Not that I know of, boss. I reckon he'd of told me if he was."

"All right. Sit down for a minute."

Carmichael said, "Right, boss," and sat down on the nearest bench.

Now Walt rose, left his bench, and slowly began to pace the kitchen. Several questions came into his mind but chief among them was how Sam or Les could have a sample of his handwriting. Every written record he'd ever kept had gone up in the fire. He had written no letters for years. He'd written Sam on the occasion of the wreck that killed his father and mother, but that letter had never been received because it was misaddressed. There was his signature on the pay checks, but that was all.

He took a slow step forward, started a second, then halted abruptly. He'd written letters to Rita when they were courting. Was it possible she had kept his letters over all these years? *It has to be that,* he thought with quiet fury. That Mexican bitch had given his letters to Sam so Sam could make trouble for him. There was no other explanation for the existence of a sample of his handwriting that was taken to the reservation.

He went back to the table and sat down again, trying to think past his fury. He ignored the silent Carmichael seated opposite him. He could confront Rita with the evidence that she had conspired to hurt him but that would mean a very risky return to Garrison. If he were seen he'd wind up in jail for breaking Cable's orders.

He was remembering now his quick flight from Garrison after Steve Palmer told him that he'd been seen at Bar D on the night of the fire. He had reached Circle P and halted just long enough to pick up a blanket roll and some grub before heading for one of the nameless canyons in the Bradburys. He found a creek, staked out his horse in the stream-bank grass, and spent a restless, near-sleepless night.

Next afternoon Carmichael had ridden in and caught him up on the gossip in Garrison. He told of Les's killing of Palmer at Bar D and the story of Palmer's deviousness. What had angered him the most was that he had broken Cable's orders to stay in town. And all for nothing. He was on the run because he had believed Palmer's story that a rider had seen him that night of the fire.

All that was done with now, Walt thought sourly. He picked up the wanted flier, read it again, and slapped it down on the table.

"That makes me crowbait, don't it?"

"Damn close to it," Carmichael said. "Anybody can kill you and claim you drew first."

Walt nodded gloomily. He slapped the reward flier and said, "Think this has hit Garrison?"

"My guess is they went off on the noon stage."

"That makes you my errand boy, Harry. I want to find out what's going on down there from Howard Olsen, but damned if I'll show up there. You will."

"When?" Carmichael said.

"Let's plan to be in the foothill timber before daylight. Want your check from me now?"

"What for?"

"You quit me. When you heard about the rustling you asked for your time. You can show my check to Olsen in case he doubts your word."

Carmichael smiled wryly. "Give it to me in the morning. I can't cash it tonight."

"If anybody's awake before I am, tell them to wake me."

Carmichael rose and said, "See you in the morning, boss."

By first light Walt and Carmichael, the latter leading a pack horse, were in the screening foothill timber of the Bradburys, headed south. Carmichael had his protective terminal check in his pocket. Their conversation was intermittent, Walt doing the talking, Carmichael making mental notes. Walt had considered and rejected having Carmichael deliver a note to Rita which would ask her to meet him somewhere outside of town. Upon last night's reflection, he was certain that Rita would refuse to meet him anywhere, especially now that he was wanted by the law.

By the time they had reached Soda Creek, where Walt had decided to make camp above the bitter water, it was early afternoon. Carmichael understood that he was to head for town immediately and hunt up lawyer Olsen, there to find out if the reward notice on Walt had reached Garrison and to find out when Rita would see him after dark in Olsen's office.

Carmichael reached Garrison a half hour later and, remembering instructions, headed for Howard Olsen's. He found the office locked and went upstreet to the saloon in Garrison House. There was only one bartender on duty and, save for a couple of strangers playing rummy at a far table, he was the only customer. Carrying his beer to a back table, he rolled a smoke and pondered his conversations with Walt last night and today. He tried to anticipate what Olsen would say in answer to his questions. The most important thing for him to learn was if the wanted dodger was out on Walt here in town and just where he and the rest of Walt's crew now stood. If Walt were brought in, would he involve all the rest of the boys in the rustling? It was too soon to tell, but he had another hole card besides his payoff check from Walt. He was the only one who knew where Walt was right now. In a pinch he could turn him in, collect the reward, and get out of the country fast.

When he went back to Olsen's office the door was unlocked, the waiting room empty. Olsen had heard the outer door close and moved through his office doorway to greet his caller. He halted, looked at Carmichael, and said, "I know you but I've forgotten the name."

Carmichael came forward and Olsen extended his hand. After shaking hands Carmichael said, "Harry Carmichael. Used to work with Walt Dana."

Olsen gave him a deliberate look and said, "Used to, past tense. That means you don't anymore?"

Harry reached into his shirt pocket and drew out Walt's check, saying, "I was paid off today. I quit." He extended the check to Olsen, who glanced at it, nodded, and returned it. He moved toward a couple of easy chairs facing a table beside his office door.

Olsen gestured, to a chair and said, "Be right with you," and went into his office. He returned immediately with the wanted flier on Walt. Halting before Carmichael, he extended it, then took the other chair by the table. Seating himself, he said, "Know anything about this?"

Carmichael didn't even bother to read it. He said,

"Yes, that's why I'm here." At Olsen's nod he continued, "Like I said, I used to work for Walt until I saw this." He tapped the wanted flier. "I didn't have anything to do with this here. I'm only a workin' puncher that took orders from the ramrod, Wiley Shores. What's goin' to happen to me and the rest of Walt's crew?"

"I can't tell you yet," Olsen said. "I just came from the sheriff's office and he won't know until Walt's brought in and charged."

"You still Walt's lawyer?" Carmichael asked.

Olsen grimaced. "I'm his lawyer of record so I guess you could say I am, although I never expected this."

Carmichael moved deeper into his chair and crossed his legs. "I haven't been in town in a week. What the hell's happening?"

Olsen told him what he already knew—that Palmer had been shot and killed by Les Beecham.

Carmichael shook his head with mock sadness. "I reckon I'm gettin' out of here at the right time." Now he came to his feet and said, "I'd like to say goodbye to Rita Dana before I leave. The name of her boarding house is Petty's, if I remember right."

"No more," Olsen said. "She's bought herself a house at the edge of town and has already moved in."

Carmichael's surprise was genuine. "How do I find it?"

"Same street as Petty's and same side, last house, a two-room log cabin. Sam moved her in yesterday."

"You mean Walt bought her the house? I thought he was through with her for good."

"Part of her support money from Walt. New court order from O'Hara. She's still married to Walt and is entitled to support."

"She still workin' for Safford's Dry Goods?"

"She quit yesterday," Olsen said. "She's opening a dressmaking shop in her house."

Carmichael had learned what he was sent to find out and now he extended his hand, which Olsen accepted. "Much obliged, Mr. Olsen. I'll tell Walt you're still workin' for him. Is that right?"

"When it is necessary, I will," Olsen said. "Tell Walt to stay out of town but to keep in touch with me. Where can I reach him in a hurry?"

"Circle P is your best bet. One of the crew'll know where to find him."

When he mounted his horse the town was in the shade of the hulking Bradburys and the streets were mostly empty. He turned right on the street past Petty's Boarding House, where the lamps were already lit against the dusk. The fourth house beyond Petty's where the street petered out into a road was Rita Dana's two-room log shack. The lamps were lit in both rooms and he could see her moving past the window in the north room.

Since there was no reason for him to go further he turned his horse around and headed toward the foothills for Walt's camp.

On his ride to it he reviewed what he'd learned from Olsen that afternoon. It seemed to him that Walt Dana was headed for big trouble and he wondered if he himself wasn't due for part of that trouble too. If it came and he was stuck with Circle P it was worth more than the fifty-five dollars a month he was getting paid. He'd observed after watching men in a bind that when trouble came they were usually willing to pay to avoid it. Surely Walt was paying Olsen a good fee to protect and defend him.

He had that in mind as he headed up the wooded shore of Soda Creek. He did not smell smoke until he saw the tiny, hooded fire on the creek bank where the evening updraft from the plains dispersed it.

From the timber a voice called, "Sing out. Who is it?"

"Carmichael, boss," Harry called. He let his horse

drink from the clean stream as Walt came out of the darkening timber afoot and a rifle in his hands. He came up to Carmichael and said, "Don't offsaddle until we talk, Harry. I may need you again tonight."

Walt jumped the narrow creek and headed for the fire, and now Carmichael pulled his horse around and dismounted just short of the fire and tied his horse to a low spruce tree. The chill of the coming night prompted Carmichael to untie and put on his duck jacket before he moved to the fire, Walt now seated beside it. There was a coffeepot on the fire and Walt filled two cups from it, handed Harry one, took the other, and sat down on the grassy creek bank. "Word out in town?" Walt asked.

Carmichael hunkered down by the fire and said, "You betcha'."

"What does Olsen think?" Walt asked.

"He don't like it. But there's nothing for him to do until you're caught and charged."

"See Rita?"

"You said not to, but she's still in town." Carmichael went on to tell of Rita's new house beyond her old boarding house. Sam had moved her in yesterday and the lamps in her new house were lit this evening. He'd seen her at a distance through the window.

Walt sat in scowling silence as Carmichael finished and took a swig of his coffee. When Walt spoke next it was sourly. "Olsen say where Rita got the money to buy a new house?"

"He said somethin' about a court order from O'Hara on you for her support."

"He fought it, didn't he?" Walt demanded.

"Don't sound like it," Harry said. "She bought the house and quit her job at Safford's."

"That coffee-colored bitch will bust me," Walt growled.

"Well, women ain't like a horse. You only have to feed him, but a woman you gotta feed, dress, and shelter."

"Ever try it?" Walt asked sourly.

Carmichael drained his cup and tossed the dregs into the fire. "Nope. Never could afford it, but I reckon you can."

Walt looked stonily at him. "How do you figure that?"

Carmichael said in a level tone of voice, "You steal beef and sell it to a crooked Indian agent."

Walt's ruddy face flushed darker. "You should know," he said with heavy sarcasm. "You keep an eagle for yourself out of every bit of cash Baines sends me by you."

"I take the risk you was afraid to."

"And who are they lookin' for now, you or me?"

Carmichael rose deliberately and when he was standing his six-gun was out of its holster and pointed at Walt.

Walt said with a surprising mildness for him, "What are you after, Harry?"

"What everybody's after," Carmichael said. "More money. I can boss your hardcase crew. I can lick any man in it and I can be picked up by the law anytime, all for fifty-five dollars a month. It's not enough."

Walt said slowly, "Seems to me I paid you off this mornin'."

"You just think you did," Carmichael said. "Double my wages or I go to Ransome, Munson, and Cable right now. Under this gun you're already worth a hundred dollars to me."

"Your wages are already doubled. Now put that gun up."

"Thanks for your generous offer to double my pay," Carmichael said with heavy sarcasm. "As for the gun, it stays where it is. You're a changeable man until you've got time to think about it, so think about it while I get me back to the spread."

Carmichael, gun still leveled, backed off to his horse, untied it, and swung into the saddle. Walt's rifle lay on the bank beside him, Carmichael knew, and now he said, "Get up and jump the creek where I can see you. Before you jump, drop your pistol in the creek. It'll dry out."

Walt rose, moved down to the creek, drew his gun and tossed it into the water, and jumped the narrow creek.

Carmichael was beside him as he climbed the opposite bank. Without a word Carmichael put spurs to his horse and headed north through the timber. It was so close to dark that Carmichael had to swerve his horse around a thicket of saplings too troublesome to ride through.

When Carmichael yanked his horse to the right, Walt jumped the creek, picked up his rifle, levered in the shell as he raised it, and tried to sight on Carmichael and could not. He knew that Carmichael, to get in a shot, had to turn in his saddle and sight from a galloping horse, a near-impossible chore in the deepening dusk.

Walt raised his rifle, could only see a blur, and shot at the sound of Carmichael's horse crashing through the brush. His bullet made a ripping sound through the timber; then there was only the sound of Carmichael's horse ramming through the small stuff.

He knew he had missed Carmichael and that by the time he could reach his own horse, tighten his cinch, and replace the bit, Carmichael would be too far away to pick up in this near-dark. Nevertheless, he recrossed the creek and found his horse.

What he could not know was that while he was getting ready to ride, Carmichael was taking off his neckerchief and bandaging the wound made in the bicep of his left arm by Walt's bullet.

Neither could he know that Carmichael now decided to head for Bar D and Sam Dana.

* * *

Headed for town now in the deep dusk, Walt went over in his mind the news Carmichael had brought him from town. While he'd been gone Rita and doubtless Sam had been working behind his back to ruin him. If Carmichael had heard rightly, and he usually did, Rita had a new house with court-awarded money—his.

Adding up her treacheries only served to rekindle his anger at and hatred of her. In effect, her letters which Sam had turned over to Ransome were responsible for the sorry mess he found himself in—on the run, money on his head, and no place to hide. She was no wife and never had been; a sour-tongued and childless shrew. This court's judgment against him was the last straw. She was no wife, no mother, no cook, no housekeeper, no companion, only the classic greedy female.

It was getting dark enough that he thought he could ride straight to Rita's new place without being recognized, but he didn't want to take the chance. Accordingly, he headed north, skirted town, met no one, and found Rita's new house without any trouble. There was a sorry frame barn and woodshed to the east of the house and he tied his horse there, then headed for the back door. Lamps were lit in both rooms but approaching the house he saw Rita in the south room, busy in the kitchen.

He did not bother to knock but opened the back door that led into the kitchen. Rita heard the door open and looked to see who her visitor was. She was at the stove, wearing an apron over a new dress Walt had never seen before. At sight of him her face hardened but she said in a friendly enough voice, "Come to see the new house, Walt?"

Walt took off his hat, pitched it onto the oilcloth-covered round table in the corner, and said, "Our new house, you mean?"

"The deed is made out to me," Rita answered.

"Have it changed. It's my money that bought it."

Rita moved two steps closer to him and looked at his surly face and smiled. "That's not what the court says. Half of what you earn a year is mine for support. Magistrate O'Hara says—"

Walt reached out to put his hand on the back of Rita's head. Instinctively she moved away from his grasp and straight into the hand-fisted left hook aimed at her jaw.

Rita, totally unprepared, took the blow under the hinge of her jaw; the savage force of it swept her off her feet and straightened her body, and she fell on her side, sliding across the floor and crashing into one of the kitchen chairs. Her body toppled it and she skidded into the far wall with savage abruptness.

"How's that for a beginning?" Walt asked softly, and headed for her.

It was close to full dark when Carmichael rode into Bar D, was picked up by a mounted lookout, and asked to see Sam Dana.

Both men dismounted at the tie rail and because the Bar D man walked ahead toward the house he did not notice that Carmichael was unsteady on his feet. At the puncher's thundering knock on the door a lamp inside was moved closer to the front window and the door was opened by Sam.

"I think we got a visitor here, boss," the puncher said. Sam opened the door wider and said, "Come in."

Carmichael went in first. His shirtsleeve, in spite of the crude tourniquet close to his shoulder, was blood-soaked.

Behind Sam, Les Beecham moved closer to the door and said, "Carmichael! What the hell did you run into?"

Sam took Carmichael's good elbow in his hand and

guided him toward the sofa and watched him sink wearily onto it.

Carmichael answered Les's question. "Walt Dana is what." He looked from Sam to Les. "I think you two better get to town right now. I think Walt's headed to town to beat up—" he corrected himself—"to make trouble for his wife. Better hurry. Take my horse.

The puncher said, "Mine too."

Both Sam and Les moved to the hat rack by the door and hurried out. Before closing the door Sam said to the puncher, "Charlie, get him a drink and look after him."

It was as fast a ride to town as the full darkness would allow and their horses, their night vision unimpaired by the lamplight in the house, set their own fast pace. In town, Sam, who knew the location of Rita's house when Les did not, took the lead.

Both rooms of Rita's new house were lamplit and as they dismounted at the front door Sam vaulted out of the saddle first and ran for the kitchen door. It was open and over its threshold lay the sprawled figure of Rita.

Sam knelt and turned her over gently. She was, they both saw, unconscious, her face swollen, her nose bleeding, and her lower jaw oddly slanted sideways. Sam said, rising, "Hand her up to me, Les. Then you ride like hell for Dr. Price's."

Sam went back to his horse, mounted, and rode the horse close to the doorway. Les lifted Rita's slim and slack figure, stood on the step, and when Sam leaned over in the saddle Les lifted Rita into his outstretched arms. Without a word Les ran for his horse, vaulted into the saddle, and headed at a gallop for Dr. Price's frame house in town.

By the time Sam had walked his horse down the main street, taken the street past Cy Allen's office, and stopped in the block beyond it, Mrs. Price had a lantern lit and was standing on the stepping block. Les and Dr. Price held a stretcher between them and now, holding it shoulder high, they moved up against Sam's horse. Very gently Sam lowered Rita onto the stretcher.

The bed in Dr. Price's one-room hospital was turned down and with Mrs. Price holding the lantern ahead of them they moved into the front bedroom and carefully lifted Rita onto it.

Dr. Price, heavyset, white-haired, and ruddy-faced, said to his slim, gray-haired wife, "You stay here and help me, Martha." To the two men he said, "Go in my waiting room, gentlemen. I'll see you when there's something to report." With a wave of his hand he indicated the door of the waiting room.

Inside the waiting room across the hall from the bedroom, both Les and Sam were on reasonably familiar ground. The furniture was old and shabby, made so by a succession of expectant fathers, worried relatives of hurt men, women, and children since long before the hospital had been built. Behind the closed door of the dimly lit waiting room, each of them sought a window to stare out into the night. They had brought in and turned over to Dr. Price a hurt and unconscious woman. How badly hurt neither of them really knew.

Sam turned, looked at Les at the front window, and asked, "Added it up?"

"Kind of," Les said. "But where does he go except into the back brush? No other place for him to hide."

"Baines's records, maybe?" Sam asked. "Ransome couldn't take them without a court order. He'd have to go to Junction City, and that would give Walt time to get to Baines."

"So the reservation is where we look for Walt?"

"Seems likely," Sam said. "He gets to Baines, pulls a gun he doesn't intend to use, and makes a bonfire of all incriminating papers in Baines's back yard. If it was your hide and you knew what papers Baines held on you, isn't that what you'd do?"

Les only nodded and started to slowly pace the worn-out rug.

The waiting-room door opened and Dr. Price came into the room, halted in the middle of it, and looked from one man to the other. It was Sam he finally addressed himself to. "What in tarnation did she tangle with? Was she pulled out of a buggy and dragged by a horse?"

"What shape's she in, Doc?" Sam countered.

"She's conscious, bruised all over like she'd been kicked, cracked jawbone and cheekbone and broken nose. What do you two know about it?"

"Only that when we rode up to her new house, the lamps were lit, the door open, and she was facedown, half in, half out of the house. The rest you know."

"I'll have to report this to Cable," the doctor said. "If we've got a maniac loose he better know about it."

"He'd better know about it tonight," Sam said. "If you'd like me to, I'll stop by his house and tell him about it. He can check with you in the morning."

"Good. I don't like to leave her now, even with Martha watching, and it'd be a favor, Sam."

"Any chance of seeing her tomorrow?"

"No, not tomorrow or the next day or the next. She needs rest and no visitors. You can't talk with her because she can't talk, so you'll have to wait a few days. If there's a change for the worse I'll get word to you. I'll tell her you found her."

Sam and Les said goodnight. Out at the stepping block, Les hauled up and waited for Sam. "You headin' for Cable?" At Sam's grunt of affirmation, he said, "I'll go back to Rita's and straighten up things. See you there."

They parted on Main Street and Sam headed reluctantly for Cable's house. This could be reckoned an official report of what they had found and Dr. Price's opinion of Rita's condition, so it could not be interpreted as a social visit. At Cable's house he ground-haltered his horse at the front gate, climbed the porch steps, and knocked. Sistie opened the door and by the light from the hall lamp she recognized him immediately.

Before she could even greet him Sam said, "Evenin', Sistie. Want to talk to your Pa. Sheriff's business, I guess you'd call it."

"Trouble, Sam?" Sistie asked.

"You could call it that," Sam said quietly. "Rita Dana's been beat up and hurt and I reckon it's sheriff's business."

Sistie opened the door wider as Sam took off his hat. As he did, Sistie said, "I'm not surprised. . . ."

The kitchen lamp was burning and the front door open when Sam rode up to Rita's house, dismounted, and went into the kitchen, where Les was seated at the kitchen table, arms folded on an open Bible. At Sam's quiet entrance Les raised his blond head from his arms and yawned as he rose.

"Know what we forgot?" Sam asked.

"Yeah, where Walt's camp is. We couldn't find it tonight anyway. Carmichael can tell us in the morning."

15

Hide yourself, man, Walt thought as he rode into his dark camp and his horse answered the whinnying greeting of the pack horse back in the trees. Common sense told him he must move camp since either Carmichael or the law would soon be here looking for him. The easiest thing to do was to head up Soda Creek, keeping to the water as long as possible, and then make camp.

An hour and a half later he gave his horse its head and let himself be carried to a grassy meadow where both horses started to feed.

He built a small fire at the edge of the timber, offsaddled his horse, unloaded the pack horse, and staked out both to graze. After a supper of bacon, bread, and coffee, he tossed Carmichael's blanket roll under a towering spruce, sat down on it, and with his back against the tree trunk attempted to sort out just exactly how much trouble he was in. He had left Rita unconscious but breathing. He had no regrets about that, since she had more than the beating coming to her. Still, she would tell what had happened to her when she was able to talk, probably to Cable. When he surfaced, that would be the least serious of the charges he would face. *A man has a right to beat up his wife if she was disloyal to him, and desertion is disloyalty. No juryman would find me guilty.*

In the stillness of his night camp he considered his situation. Marshal Ransome's reward offer would make every man he met his enemy.

He tried to sort out his problems in order of their importance. The first, obviously, was for him to stay alive. The second was to see Sam dead; by whose hand it didn't matter. With Sam dead he would inherit Bar D and whatever holdings that furnished Sam with the money he had. In short, he had to outlive Sam but not be anywhere near the scene of his death.

The most immediate problem was tomorrow. He knew Sam would get word of Rita's beating and would be on his trail immediately. What if he headed south out of this camp? Wouldn't Sam reason he was jumping the country, assuming that the reward dodger would insure his capture? Added to that, would Sam want to be very far from Rita when he seemed overwilling to help if it would hurt her husband? He rose now, stoked the fire, and went to his bedroll, his mind made up. He was running big risks but for even bigger stakes. And that satisfied him.

16

Shortly after sunup Sam and Les headed for Soda Creek. Last night on their return to Bar D, Carmichael had been fed and put to bed, half drunk but not before he had told some of the crew where Walt had been camped on Soda Creek.

Les spotted Walt's old camp first. From then on, clinging to the creek and leapfrogging each other to pick up a sign, they made short work of finding Walt's night camp in the meadow. There they split, Sam taking the right bank of the creek and Les the left. The first man to pick up the fresh warning sign was to whistle to the other.

Les had the meadow side of the creek while Sam had the timbered side. Sam rode slowly through the timber while Les bird-dogged back and forth across the knee-high grass of the open park. Sam knew that Les would come across signs of game feeding in the lush grass and would try to sort them out before identifying them and moving on.

So it was with some surprise that Sam came across some fresh horse droppings on the left bank of the stream.

It came to him then that Walt had traveled the stream since leaving camp, heading for the timbered ridge to the west. He went ahead a short way and confirmed the horse tracks in the mud of the stream bank.

Peeling off his left glove, he put two fingers in his mouth and whistled shrilly. He saw Les raise his head and now Sam pulled his horse out into the open. Les headed for him then and when they joined, Sam showed him the tracks and the droppings. Les observed wryly, "Reckon that pack horse got tired of cold feet."

With Les on the bank and Sam on the edge of the water, they picked up where Walt had left the stream, trailing his pack horse, headed south on a timbered ridge.

From then on the tracking was simple. Walt, he knew, was keeping to whatever screening cover he could find. It was Les who said it first, putting into words Sam's unspoken hunch. "Could he be headin' out of the country?"

"Well, he's not exactly headin' home," Sam agreed.

For close to two hours they followed the tracks which always sought screening timber. When they came to the downtilt of the valley cut by the Feather River, they paid more attention to the tracks. The Feather was a fast river, mostly white water, and Sam was curious to see if Walt knew it or if he'd bull through it. It was soon obvious that he did know it, for he had turned downstream and found a well-hidden ford where he crossed.

Again in the screening timber Walt had stopped, dismounted, paid some attention to the pack horse, and then had spooked him off at a run downhill. Walt's own horse's tracks headed downstream at a walk at the very end of the ford across the river and were headed back north.

Sam spoke first, "We've had a whizzer pulled on us unless he's riding the pack horse."

"If he was, his own horse would be rollin' and scratchin' his back. No sign of it. Walt rode that horse across and was headed north."

There seemed to be no reasoning in the way Walt traveled. He ignored game trails, in fact avoided them, he was simply riding in the trackless timber, keeping doggedly north. Coming into one park past noonday, Les riding ahead, they surprised a single rider watering his horse at the slough that drained the park. At sight of them the rider waved casually and Les, Sam now beside him, rode over to the lone rider. As they approached him he called, *"Buenos días,* Bar D. Picked up any sign?"

"Hi, Cady," Les said and then added, "Sign of what?"

They reined, crossed the outlet of the slough, and surveyed the lean, young puncher who was now laughing soundlessly. "The same sign you're lookin' for," he said. "Walt Dana."

"So that's why you're alone and a long way from home," Les said. "A hundred dollars beats fifty. Is that it?"

"Well, don't it?" Cady asked. "If you two catch him, fifty apiece is all you'll get."

Cady looked now at Sam and said, "Meanin' no offense, Sam, but Walt's a big target. Half us loners up this mornin' figured likewise."

"Happy huntin', Cady," Sam said dryly.

He and Les crossed the outlet of the slough and again Les, by Sam's decision, let him go ahead and immediately they were in sun-shot timber. If by any fluke they overtook Walt, he wanted Les to get the reward money for Walt. If they missed him, which was more likely, they would at least have a look at Circle P which could give a clue to Walt's whereabouts.

When they reached Circle P they paused in the closest timber and Sam took out his field glasses and glassed the house, which was shut and told him nothing.

There were no horses in the corral, none even close in the horse pasture, and only the grindstone at the far corner of the building indicated that people had once lived here.

Wordlessly Sam passed the glasses to Les, who had a long, long look.

"What do you make of it?" Sam asked.

"Looks like Walt and his crew are gone."

"I'm goin' to have a look-see."

"That's pretty damn open, Sam. I'd better go with you."

Sam, kneeling, pounded his thigh with his fist. "Makes no sense, Les. Why'd he come back?" Now Sam rose, picked up his rifle, and said, "You stay in your hidey-hole. If you see anyone moving down there let off a shot."

Sam rose and headed down the slope, taking no particular trouble to move quietly. Once he was on the flats and in the open, he moved into a jog, headed for the shallow porch and front door.

From somewhere up on a close hill came the sound of a shot and a geyser of dust blossomed in front of him. The shot was followed immediately by a second shot, which Sam reckoned was Les sound-shooting the rifleman.

Sam made the porch in his final charge, halted only long enough to raise a booted foot and drive it into the front door. It sprang open with a crash and he lunged into the big living room. Without a pause except to slam the door closed behind him, he moved into the corridor that led to the kitchen. Brushing aside the curtain to the room on his left, he saw that the bed was unmade and clothes were strewn about the room. The room opposite was even more untidy. In the big kitchen, unwashed cups and plates were still on the big table. There were two more rifle shots from the hill outside, one of which broke the window of the bedroom closest to the hill. The third shot, a prompt answer, was from Les.

Sam halted in the corridor just short of the kitchen and made a dismal assessment of the situation. Obligingly, in his mule-headed stubbornness, he had walked into the trap Walt had designed for him. It was only a matter of

time before Walt and his crew chased Les off or gunned
him down. As if echoing his thoughts, he heard a steady
fusillade of shots from the hill, none of which were aimed
at the house.

He moved back into the bedroom closest to the hill,
looked out the broken window, and saw a movement up
the slope. He poked his rifle out the window and fired
two quick shots at a moving target among the trees. At
horse or man, he didn't know.

Cady, following a game trail and headed south, heard
the first shot. The third shot was louder than the first
two, meaning that the gun was pointed at the mountain
which was now in afternoon shade.

There was no mistaking where the shooting was taking
place, for it had to be Circle P. He turned his horse and
headed angling down through the timber.

Further up the mountain and a ridge up behind Cady,
two riders heard the shots. They exchanged looks without saying anything. They both turned their horses
downslope and in the direction from which the shots
came.

Further north from these two riders, a single rider
picked up the sound of distant gunfire below. He too left
a game trail and headed downslope.

A fifth rider reined in at the sound of continuing gunfire down below, halted his horse and pack mule and
wondered what kind of hell was breaking loose down on
the flats. He was a prospector and a stranger to this
county. Sustained shooting like that meant trouble and
he wanted no part of it. He headed uphill again, glad he
wasn't down below.

Still further north, a pair of young riders out for buck-
skin heard the distant firing. Somebody, they thought,
had spooked a herd of elk, but without saying so to each

other they knew that wasn't true. Elk at this time of year would be in the highest grassy parks; but, curious at the volume of gunfire, they headed downslope.

Walt, farthest up the hill, was the first to hear Cady's horse. He led his horse downslope to a side canyon to where his men and their horses on the ridge that had a view of the house were strung out. Fred Beasley, mounted, was the horse guard.

Walt reined in beside him and said, "Someone's comin' down the canyon. I'll cut around down to the barn. Now listen to this careful, will you?" At Beasley's curt nod he said, "It's not Sam in the house, it's me. You haven't been paid in two months, so you're bounty huntin' too. Got that?"

"It's you we're shooting at. Sure."

There was isolated shooting from the crew on the ridge and Walt rode his horse through the timber along the back of the canyon and was lost from sight.

Beasley whistled shrilly and waved the crew to him. As they trailed in to him he looked up the brush-choked canyon and could hear but not see sounds of an approaching horse.

Briefly, tersely, he passed on Walt's message. It was Walt in the house, not Sam, and they had been driven to bounty hunting because of no pay in two months.

As the crew was breaking up, headed to the ridge, again Beasley looked over his shoulder and saw Cady on the canyon's shady sideslope, headed for him.

The firing by the crew along the ridge started up again. It was intermittent and sporadic, for every man knew that it was time to conserve his powder.

At Cady's approach on the canyon floor, Beasley moved his horse to face him in the lowering dusk.

"Sounds like a war goin' on down here. What's all the shooting for?"

"We're tryin' to flush Walt out of the shack, but he's stubborn," Beasley said.

The expression on Cady's face was one of mild bewilderment. "I thought you worked for him, Fred."

"Did work," Beasley said. "No pay for goin' on two months."

"Why not ride out? What's keepin' you here?"

"We need a little leavin' money, even if it ain't much."

An expression of contempt came into Cady's face. "Ten bucks a man not much more. You boys *are* hungry."

"Sure, we'll take him to court but first we gotta catch him."

"Let's see you do it," Cady said. "I got time to watch."

In the falling darkness Walt knew he had waited too long to put any distance between himself and Sam. In cold fact the coming of dark would work in Sam's favor. He was protected by the log walls. He could shoot at anything he could see and still be safe from hostile gunfire. That fire was even more sporadic now for Sam was withholding fire. *Out of ammunition?* Walt wondered. He doubted it for Sam had been firing only his rifle. That left his six-gun with a belt full of shells for any close attack.

Now Walt dismounted in the almost dark, tied his horse, reloaded his rifle and, standing at the edge of the timber, tried to make out the outlines of the buildings that lay almost below him and now, rifle in hand, he left the timber and headed for the rear of the barn. At the empty corral he opened a gate, walked to the stable, and tramped through the doorway at the end of the manger into the barn proper. The wagon doors were open and again from memory he skirted a hulking chuck wagon and headed for an unlit lantern hanging on the door frame. Taking down the lantern, he carried it in his left hand and headed for the house.

The rifle fire from the hill had quieted, for now in the almost full dark nothing around the house could be seen clearly from the hill.

A sense of urgency was upon him. If he could barely see the house, then from the house Sam could barely see the barn. This was the time for Sam to clear out before somebody thought of setting fire to the house.

Moving out into the coming night, he headed for the side of the house farthest from the hill. He did not know if he could be seen from either the hill or the house, but he had no choice but to head for the side of the house away from the hill. When he made its corner without drawing fire he halted, let his breathing slow down, and then headed for the kitchen's side window. What he planned he knew was risky, but not so risky as entering through the back door and hunting down Sam room by dark room. At the kitchen window he knelt and struck a match, making no attempt to light the lantern. He held the match up against the window.

Nothing happened and as the match began to scorch his fingers he dropped it. His next move was toward the window of the east bedroom, where he again kept out of sight but held the match until the flame gutted out, again making no attempt to light the lantern.

That left the window of the living room.

Sam, unless he was a fool, would be backed up against the east wall of the living room, away from the searching rifle bullets from the hill.

Now Walt knelt, the lantern between his knees, un-screwed the cap from the lantern's base, and sloshed the coal oil around until it soaked the base of the lantern. Afterward he turned up the wick, struck a match, lighted the wick, rose, and hurled the lantern through the east window. Almost instantly on impact, the spilled coal oil was aflame, the lantern inside the room.

"Run or burn, Sam," Walt shouted.

Les, already on his way to the east side of the house, heard Walt's shouted order and only then broke into a run, rifle in hand.

He had not yet reached the corner of the porch when he heard the close blast from a rifle. Rounding the corner of the porch, he saw Walt illuminated by the flames from the lantern inside.

As Les lifted his rifle to his shoulder, Walt levered another shell in the chamber and started to sight. The bullet from Les's rifle caught Walt on the flat side of his head. It knocked him down and as he fell on his side he was already dead.

17

Sam and Les parted on Garrison's dark Main Street. Les headed for Cable's house to report his killing of Walt. Sam looked up the sidestreet and saw that Dr. Price's office lamp was burning brightly. The bedroom where Sam had left Rita was only dimly lit by a night lamp.

"See you at the hotel," Sam said.

"Yeah, with a bottle," Les answered.

They parted and Sam rode up the sidestreet past Cy's dark office. After the fire had been put out at Circle P, Sam had refused to listen to Fred Beasley's explanation of Walt's last deception. There was more urgent business here in town with Rita.

Sam put his horse in at Dr. Price's stepping block, tied his horse there, and strode up the brick walk, mounted the steps, and knocked thunderously on the half-glassed door. Through the curtains he saw Dr. Price, carrying a lamp, move toward the door and open it.

Dr. Price was in shirtsleeves, his collar off, and he gave Sam only the barest of nods.

"You tryin' to wake up the town?" he asked angrily.

"I've got to see Rita, right now," Sam said gruffly.

"She's asleep, or was until you tried to kick down the door."

"Then go wake her, or shall I?"

Dr. Price opened the door wider and said grouchily, "Oh, come in then, damn it. I'll wake her."

He turned, went down the hall a few feet, and, without bothering to knock, opened the door.

Rita lay half propped up in bed, her dark hair cascading over her shoulders. She was awake and when she saw Sam she lifted her right hand and wiggled her fingers in silent greeting.

Sam yanked off his hat and moved past Dr. Price to her bedside and halted. There was no easy way to say what must come, only it had to be said. He spoke gently now. "Rita, Walt's dead, shot to death. He never knew what happened to him."

A look of surprise, almost shock, came into Rita's bruised and swollen face. Instinctively she made the sign of the cross.

"By you?" Dr. Price growled.

Sam turned his head and looked at him. "Not by me," he said. "It could have been, but it wasn't. Now, could you leave us alone, Doc? I've got something important to say to Rita but I want to say it to her alone."

"Don't be long. If you are, I'll be back," Dr. Price said. He went out, closing the door behind him.

"I'm a damned grim messenger," Sam said. "But I'd rather tell you than have Parker or Cable come over and ask you where you want him buried."

Rita looked away, picked up a handkerchief from the spread, and dabbed at her eyes.

Tears for a dead man, not for her husband, Sam thought. When she looked at him again Sam said, "I'm going to ask you some questions. If the answer is yes nod your head up and down. If the answer is no move your head from side to side." He paused. "Ready?"

Rita moved her head up and down in assent.

"How long is Doc Price going to keep you here? In weeks, I mean?"

Without even thinking Rita raised her right hand with three fingers upright and then shrugged.

"If you're lucky, you mean." At Rita's nod, Sam went on, "He'll want you close to town for a while, won't he?"

At Rita's nod, he said, "Bar D's not too far from town for a soft ride in a buggy. Sound good?"

Rita nodded affirmatively.

Sam reached out and gently touched her swollen face. "It better, because that's where you'll be living the rest of your life."